So Many Unavoidable Journeys

Palewell Press

So Many Unavoidable Journeys

Prose Anthology

So Many Unavoidable Journeys

First edition 2025 from Palewell Press,
www.palewellpress.co.uk

Printed and bound in the UK

ISBN 978-1-911587-77-4

All Rights Reserved. Copyright © 2025 Palewell Press. No part of this publication may be reproduced or transmitted in any form or by any means, without permission in writing from the publisher.

Copyright to each individual piece remains with the contributors: Pingala Dhital; Sharif Gemie; Marsha Glenn; Fatima Hagi; Anba Jawi; dima mekdad; Nasrin Parvaz; Haydeh Ravesh; and Michael Tanner.

The right of the contributors to be identified as the authors of their work has been asserted by them in accordance with the Copyright, Designs and Patents Act 1988

For privacy reasons, some names, locations, and dates may have been changed.

The front-cover vector image was downloaded from our image suppliers at www.shutterstock.com and is Copyright © 2025 Sebos

The cover design is Copyright © 2025 Camilla Reeve

A CIP catalogue record for this title is available from the British Library.

Acknowledgements

Sincere thanks to Esme Edwards for co-editing this anthology with me, and to the contributors for the honesty and courage with which they shared their stories.

Dedication

This book is dedicated to all those who, facing impossible conditions in their original home, or ejected from it by hostile action, dare to seek a new place to live.

Contents

Introduction 3

It feels like once upon a time... 4

Social Activist Versus Motherhood 24

Love and Shame 38

Oracle 52

The Calligraphy Class 62

The Farmer's Daughter 74

Her Two Scars 81

Every Black Rock... 87

Dreaming Beneath the Asmara Sun 104

Contributor Biographies 112

There is no greater agony than bearing an untold story inside you. **Maya Angelou**

Introduction

Most of us want nothing more than to get on with our lives and see our children grow up safe and happy. But what if nation or nature conspires against us, if we're being shot at, tortured or starved by drought? We may feel forced to leave. Forced displacement within one's own country or having to cross into other countries currently impacts 1 in 67 people.

Becoming a migrant is never an easy choice but a profoundly sad and complex one, born of desperation. What must it be like to leave everything behind – familiar landscapes, the mother tongue, valid professional qualifications, contact with best friends, the closeness needed to care for aging family members. Taking such a decision, and the journey that follows it, must irrevocably change a person. That migration becomes a defining act in their life story.

It helps people to share stories, to explain to others and sometimes to themselves as well, why it was vital to leave, how the journey went, and what was encountered in the new place. After trauma, having one's experiences witnessed is part of the healing process. In this anthology, Palewell Press is bearing witness to stories that meant a lot to those involved and will resonate with others who faced similar challenges. As James Baldwin wrote: "Generations do not cease to be born, and we are responsible to them because we are the only witnesses they have." We invite you to travel with us on *So Many Unavoidable Journeys*.

It feels like once upon a time...

Memoir by Pingala Dhital

My name is Pingala Dhital. I was born in 1972 in Hilley village, Sarpang district, Bhutan. I lived with my grandparents, parents, and four younger brothers. I am the eldest and the only girl in my family. My grandparents had lived in Bhutan since the early 1900s.

In November 1990, when I was 17 years old, I left my home in Southern Bhutan to cross the border to the nearest Indian village for what I thought would be two weeks. I have never been able to return. We expected to come back when the political situation had cooled down after big political demonstrations in our area. Yet, after spending nine months in India, my family was driven by bus to the Nepal/India border. While we lived in a refugee camp in Nepal for 18 years, we longed to return home to Bhutan. Even now, when I have built a home in the United States (US), where I was resettled in 2008, not a single day passes without a deep yearning to see my birthplace again.

There are three main ethnic groups in Bhutan - the Ngalong, Sharchops, and Lhotshampas. The Ngalong group occupies the western part of the country and the royal family belongs to this group. They are of Tibetan origin and follow Mahayana Buddhism. The Sharchops, who are of Indo Mongoloid origin, live in the eastern part of the country. The Lhotshampas, meaning "southern border landers" are the Bhutanese people of Nepalese descent. They settled in southern Bhutan from the late 1800s to the early 1900s. The majority of them follow Hinduism.

Following a census in 1979-1981, the Bhutanese government grew concerned about the Lhotshampa population. In 1988, The government conducted another census only in the south, requiring citizens to produce a 1958 land tax receipt to prove their citizenship. Subsequently, individuals were classified into various categories, including illegal immigrants, if they failed to produce a 1958 receipt.

In the mid-1980s, the government of Bhutan adopted a "One Nation, One People" policy to strengthen national unity and promote harmony. This policy required all Bhutanese citizens, regardless of their ethnic background, to wear one national dress, speak one language, and work together for the common good of the nation. As part of this policy, Nepali language was removed from the school curriculum, speaking Nepali was banned on school premises, and national dress was made mandatory in common places such as market areas, schools, and offices.

In 1987, I heard about the "One Nation One People policy" being introduced in Bhutan. Our school dress was changed from a shirt and skirt to *Gho* and *Kira* (traditional Drukpa dresses worn by people in the north, where it is colder than in the south). Nepali language was removed from the school curriculum. We were no longer allowed to speak Nepali at school. As children, we were happy about the removal of Nepali language to have one less subject to study.

One day, the new *Driglam Namzha* (northern Bhutanese code of etiquette and dress) teacher pulled my long ponytail and scolded me, telling me to come back with short hair. The same afternoon, my mom and I went to a barber since there were no hair salons for women. We asked for a haircut like a boy, so my hair changed from waist-length to neck-length. I felt part of my identity was snatched in that moment as I grew up believing that women must keep their hair long. One Saturday I was taken to the police camp because I was wearing my old school dress, a skirt and a shirt. The dress was allowed on Saturdays, but I didn't know it was prohibited in public areas. Some people resisted the policy by not wearing national dress.

We heard about the arrest of many southern Bhutanese people including Tek Nath Rizal, one of the Royal Advisory councillors from the south. In June 1990, the Bhutan People's Party (BPP) announced the formation of their political group by beheading two government officials from the south. This warned the public of the consequences for anyone who refused to join them. They hung the heads under a bridge with a note in red ink threatening the same fate for government supporters. They asked villagers for support - financially and physically - and made it mandatory for every household to send a member to join them. The BPP coerced villagers to participate in anti-government demonstrations through threats and intimidation, leading to thousands of people joining the protests whether they wanted to or not.

Some other organisations, which had formed prior to the BPP, were also working together to appeal to the king, but had no plans for demonstrations or violent activities. These organisations were the Students Union of Bhutan (1988) and the People's Forum for Human Rights (1989).

One day in early September 1990, some BPP members from our village came to our house. As they discussed plans for a demonstration, one of the leaders was playing with a handgun. Accidentally, a bullet was fired narrowly missing my mother. The memory still shakes me. My mom froze with a tray of teacups in her hand, the rest of us panicked in fear in total silence. A few minutes later we heard an army truck approaching. The men thought it was because of the sound of the bullet firing so they ran away.

On September 21 1990, people from nearby villages including Deurali, Sisti, Bisti, and Singhi, gathered at a rice mill under a large blue banner that read "Long Live Our King." My friend Deepa and I held each end of the banner. My father made sure nobody had weapons, and he urged everyone to remain peaceful and respectful during our march. Many men carried *khukuris*, our traditional knives, which they left at the rice mill before we marched towards the Dzong, the district administrative office. As we marched, we chanted slogans like "release Tek Nath Rizal", "long live the BPP", and others chanted after us. When we reached a checkpoint near the river, the authorities stopped us.

The Dzongda, the district head, approached us and inquired about our intentions. My father explained we wanted to visit the Dzong and present the BPP's 13-point demand appeal to the king. The Dzongda kindly offered us to take rest and water from a tap. He went back to his office to contact authorities in Thimphu and later returned, suggesting that we could hand over the appeal and return home to avoid the scorching sun. However, the group was determined to proceed to the Dzong. After further deliberation, we were granted permission to march on. We crossed the bridge and walked about 3 km to the Dzong. We respectfully encircled the King's photo, bowing in reverence. My dad handed over the appeal to the authorities and departed peacefully. I never found out the exact contents of the appeal but the memory of that day remains vivid in my mind.

Two days later on 23rd September 1990, the Dzongda called my father to his house and shared worries about public safety. He recounted the escalating violence by the BPP members in our village. They were confiscating national dresses and burning them on the streets. Whereas our demonstration was very peaceful, we heard that the demonstrators in other districts were violent and that BPP members brought weapons and clashed with police officers. Some protesters burned national dresses and blocked roads.

In October 1990, my great uncle was kidnapped because he could not pay the BPP 30,000 Bhutanese Ngultrum donation My grandfather rushed to the jungle, paid the money, and brought him back home. Later, the kidnappers went back to my great uncle's house twice and stole everything. Not a penny was left behind. In our culture, it is customary to place a silver coin on the dead's forehead, so my great uncle had saved over a hundred of these coins. Although people exchanged cash in hard times, they would always save enough coins for their death. However, when my great uncle died, the family could not find one silver coin for his forehead.

The same month, my friend's young husband was kidnapped and never came back. There is no record or mention of him anywhere. Later, we heard from some people in Saralpara that he was kidnapped from his home by members of the BPP. He was taken to India and buried alive after both of his eyes were stabbed. I still wonder why he became the victim of such a heinous crime. Was it because he belonged to a different ethnic group, or did the BPP members had personal issues with him. He belonged to either the Ngalong or Sharchops ethnicity but married to a Southern Bhutanese woman. Like this, the BPP terrorised the southern Bhutanese villagers in various ways.

One day, a lady we called Amai, spoke in hushed tones and shared a disturbing story about a young girl, who was raped by the BPP in our village. She was younger than me and the news was difficult to believe. There is a saying that "you can hide anything, but fear has no hiding place." I felt profoundly vulnerable, my body was chilled with goosebumps. I started imagining myself in a similar situation, if not from the BPP, then from the army.

As the demonstrations continued in Bhutan, the government began cracking down on what they considered 'anti-nationals' from southern Bhutan. The government deployed the army and police personnel in the south, resulting in widespread arrests, detentions, rapes, and torture.

The jungle began to feel like a safer place to sleep than our own home, so we went there to spend nights. It was challenging to sleep in the jungle due to the ants, the rustling of dry leaves and the constant light flashing from the police camp above as if they were looking at us.

Leaving home to return after two weeks:

One morning, as we were heading home from our hiding place in the jungle, our village representative was waiting outside our house. He seemed worried and told us to leave the village as the government was looking for my father and could arrest him at any time. He warned it could be dangerous for all of us if they did. He advised us not to hide in the jungle anymore and suggested contacting our father to find a safer place for our family to stay until things calmed down. However, a few days after the demonstration my father had left for a pilgrimage trip to get recommendations from his guru about the situation.

My mother packed some beaten rice for us and instructed my 13-year-old brother and I to go to the nearest Indian village where our dad had gone. She told us to follow the man, who helped by arranging cows to accompany us, making it seem like we were herding them to avoid attracting attention.

I hurriedly put on my favorite pink pants, rolling them up above my knees to hide them under my blue skirt (my old school dress), and layered my favorite top beneath an old white school shirt. My brother and I followed the man, whom we politely called uncle, through the fields of our almost-ready-to-harvest rice crop, unaware that it would be our last walk here. I trailed my right hand over the rice plants, feeling the gentle pricks from the grains.

We arrived safely at the Indian family's home in Saralpara, Assam, two kilometres away from our home in Bhutan where our father had been staying, but found he had gone to a different village to attend a Satsang (a religious gathering). The same night, my mother arrived with my two youngest brothers to make sure we were safe, while our grandma stayed behind. On my mother's way back home the next day, she saw many soldiers coming towards India from Bhutan. She ran back across the river to the Indian village. She recalls it as the fastest run of her life. The soldiers later raided the BPP camps in the Indian jungle and some houses in the village. A week passed, and we waited anxiously for news that we could return home. Rather we ended up traveling 20 miles south to a new village called

Jharbari in Assam. Our family decided to separate and live with different families to ease the burden on them.

Weeks became months and after we had spent five months in Jharbari, other Bhutanese people began arriving by the hundreds.

My mom decided to return to Saralpara so that all our family could live together. A lady offered us a room when we agreed to look after her cows. We lived there for another four months and on the evening of August 23rd, 1991, the Indian village headman informed us that we should pack our essentials and get ready to go to Nepal. They said it should be for six months.

The following morning of August 24th 1991, they boarded women and children on a bus to Nepal with Assam policemen on board. The policemen disembarked from the bus on the Bengal border and our dad and the other men got on the bus. We continued our journey through West Bengal towards Nepal. Our grandma was left behind at home in Bhutan.

Refugee camp

It was around 4 pm on 24th August 1991 that our bus pulled over by the side of the road in Nepal at the Maidhar riverbank camp. Someone gestured towards the bamboo huts indicating this is where we would be staying. The plastic roofs were flapping, and dust filled the atmosphere. I couldn't hold back my tears. I cried uncontrollably, overwhelmed by the feeling of the end of our normal lives. The idea of spending even one night in such a place was unimaginable. It was very sad to realize that I had left my home to become a refugee.

Soon after we arrived in Nepal, someone brought our grandmother from Bhutan. Despite her effort to save our home/ancestral land and her wish to die in the same place as her husband, she left home to be with us.

On 18th September 1992, a year after our arrival in Nepal, we were moved to Beldangi-II camp with the help of the UNHCR. The people in the camp increased every day until there were 105,000 people living in seven refugee camps in Jhapa and Morang districts by the end of 1993. I began managing Non-Formal Education classes for adults through Oxfam GB and Bhutanese Refugee Women Forum (BRWF), where I got to work with PhD students as a research assistant and help interpret for visitors from Western countries.

By 1998, I had become a mother of two children and at the end of this year, my grandma passed away. The reality of her passing hit me hard, making me realize that the cycle of life never stops.

I met my husband, Kamal, in Assam, India in December 1990. Although we are from the same village, we had never met in person before. Then I saw him again in Nepal. He was very actively involved with the Student Union of Bhutan. Since he was alone, he lived with us most of the time while he was in the camp. We got married in March 1994 and welcomed our first child a year later. Just three years later, my second child was born under the blazing heat of a plastic roof. Within minutes of birth, my newborn daughter developed a fever, needing Tylenol syrup and I fainted. As I regained consciousness, I heard my mother's voice laced with anguish, calling my name.

Every summer my children developed heat boils, red painful bumps all over their body and we spent nights fanning them with cardboard. Winters were cold under the plastic roof, even though we covered the bamboo walls with old newspaper to keep warm using cooked flour paste, which also attracted cockroaches. We often woke up with cockroach bites on our bodies. It is very hard to imagine those days now.

We still had great hopes of returning home as talks between the governments of Bhutan and Nepal were underway. On the other side, life in the camp was deteriorating. Some aid organisations were pulling out due to donor fatigue as the years went on.

After 15 rounds of bilateral talks, Nepal and Bhutan formed a Joint Verification Team (JVT) to screen the refugees to determine the number of genuine Bhutanese citizens. On 24th January 2001, the Bhutanese JVT arrived in Damak and they visited our camp on the 26th in the afternoon. I saw many Bhutanese refugees greeting them with smiles including my husband.

The joint verification process started on 26th March 2001 with 10 families from the Khudunabari camp. Unfortunately, the process did not last long because on December 23rd 2003, the Bhutanese side of the team were violently attacked by the refugees in the Khudunabari camp office. Sadly, this incident led to a standstill in bilateral talks. With this incident, our hopes to return home were shattered.

One afternoon in 2001, my 7-year-old son came back from camp school and tossed his bag containing a thin notebook and pencil and a jute rag. He ran off to play with other children in the camp. I remembered my own school days in Bhutan; a well set up school, well-trained teachers and good textbooks. It was evident to me how far behind our lives as refugees had taken us. We spent sleepless nights caring for our sick daughter. She suffered from severe pneumonia episodes with the smoky and polluted environment in the camp. I realized that we could no longer be held captive here with false hopes of return.

I began worrying about the future of my children and started to think about what to do and where to start. I had never used a computer. My husband created an email address for me and I used internet cafes in the nearby town of Damak to contact my friends in Europe seeking their advice and support. A good friend of mine in the UK helped my children study in India by sending money. In February 2002, I moved to Kalimpong, India with my husband and children.

After a few months in Kalimpong, my husband received calls from friends requesting him to work as office secretary with TN Rizal, for the Human Rights Council of Bhutan (HRCB). My husband started working for him at first in India and then later in Nepal.

In early 2004, on his usual visit home to us in Kalimpong, Kamal said there was no longer a possibility of returning home to Bhutan. Hearing that destroyed my hopes. I was stunned. There was no option to stay long-term in India and life in the refugee camp was horrible. We were stateless and our children had no future. My husband said: "now you have to speak up because our political leaders will not resolve our situation for us."

That evening, I contacted my friend Ganga to ask if she was ready to work with me. She said she would if I moved to Kathmandu, where she lived. When we went to the camp during the children's school holidays, I met with many women to talk about solving the refugee problem and they encouraged me further. I met some UNHCR officials in the camp office, including their Durable Solutions Officer, Kimberly Robertson, to learn about what was in their mandate for solving our refugee issue. This inspired me to take action.

When I came to the camp, I reconnected with women whom I'd worked with in the 90s. In October 2004, when we were in the camp to celebrate our festival, Dasain, the US Assistant Secretary of State for the Bureau of Population, Refugees, and Migration, Gene Dewey visited our camp. A Bhutanese refugee representative organisation had written an appeal to solve our refugee problem. I stood outside the hall with my own and other children from our camp sector, holding placards. The camp secretary picked up my 6-year-old daughter and took her inside the hall, where she handed the appeal to Mr. Gene Dewey. When she returned, she was shouting in excitement, "I met the King!" Through the placards the children expressed their desire to have a better future. A long banner on the side of the road read, "Help us find a durable solution, 14 years is too much in the refugee camp". It was clear to me that many people living here wanted to leave.

Later in 2004, my husband arranged for us to meet TN Rizal in Kathmandu. It was the first time I had met him. I asked him if we would be going home any time soon and told him that fifteen days had become fifteen years. He said it was a good question, but he had no good answer. Instead, he suggested that I join a Nepali women's group and work for women's rights here.

In January 2005, I moved to Kathmandu to join my husband. With support from my husband and friends, Ganga and I founded an organization, Voice for Change. Tewa Nepal and Global Fund for Women provided initial funding and support for our operations. We appealed to the Bhutanese refugee leaders and organisations to work together to solve the refugee problem first and continue to work with the political issues in Bhutan afterwards. We appealed to the Nepali Home and Foreign Ministries and to foreign diplomats to do the same.

I vividly remember our initial meeting with Nepali diplomats at the Foreign Ministry. My emotions were overwhelming leaving me speechless with tears. Despite my struggle to find words, the officer, who was part of the bilateral talks team, showed kindness and understanding. Thereafter, I gradually began to meet diplomats at different embassies including the US.

In 2006, the US Government announced an offer to resettle over 60,000 Bhutanese refugees. I heartily welcomed this offer during a press conference in October 2006 held in Birtamod, Jhapa district, Nepal. Consequently, I faced threats from Bhutanese political groups including Tek Nath Rizal and the Bhutanese Communist Party (BCP), who did not support resettlement. Instead, the BCP was inspired by the success of the Maoist movement in Nepal and wanted to fight their way back to Bhutan and force political change there.

In April 2007, I was approached by distressed women in the camp who tearfully shared that Bhutanese Maoist groups were demanding their sons to join them. Their pleas resonated deeply with me as they expressed leaving their homes in Bhutan to protect their children, not to face such peril again. Driven by their concerns, I left for Kathmandu the following day.

I went to TN Rizal's home with my husband. I relayed the women's worrying accounts to Rizal and his wife. To my astonishment, his wife suggested a dual approach for a movement; peaceful appearance on one side and violence on the other, gesturing a sign of a gun. Rizal tacitly assented. Shocked by this response, I questioned the use of violence, particularly as a mother. The dialogue continued, culminating in my inquiry about whether they would subject their own sons to such demands. Awkwardly, this marked the end of our discussion. This exchange left me deeply concerned, foreseeing a potential resurgence of the violent events of 1990 in Bhutan.

On June 20th 2007, I was interviewed by a BBC reporter, Charles Haviland, during a sit-in protest staged in front of the UN building in Kathmandu. The article, featuring my photograph, was published in the Kantipur newspaper. In the interview, I expressed our willingness to explore alternative solutions to our situation including resettlement. The next day, my husband received a call from TN Rizal issuing an ultimatum: either present me at their meeting for *bhoutik karbahi* (a Maoist term for physical punishment) or face termination of his employment. It was a dilemma - the minimal amount he was receiving was our means of survival in Kathmandu. On the other hand, he was being asked to hand me over to be physically harmed. His employment was terminated.

In August 2007, I was invited to participate in a women's conference in Thailand organized by Development Alternatives with Women for a New Era (DAWN) Southeast Asia. As I was arranging travel documents for this event, my world was shattered when my camp hut was violently attacked and destroyed. Luckily, I was not present, as the perpetrators had intended to harm me. Tragically, my family members were physically assaulted including my pregnant sister-in-law and my mother. My parents, brothers, sisters-in-law, and young nieces and nephews were now terrified and homeless.

While I was stepping out of the Home Ministry office, my father called me and recounted the horrifying events that had unfolded at our refugee camp. He revealed that he had been taken away by armed individuals to the camp office hall. There, he witnessed the brutal beating of the camp secretary from Beldangi III, who also supported resettlement, and was left bloodied and injured. They demanded my father stay put until their return, leaving him unaware of the welfare and whereabouts of our other family members.

I then received a call from the same official at the Home Ministry, whom I had just seen moments earlier. He conveyed that due to an order from our leader, Tek Nath Rizal, the Nepal government had been instructed to halt the processing of my travel documents, effectively preventing me from leaving the country. Overwhelmed with confusion and distress, I struggled to comprehend the gravity of the situation.

The next day we discovered that an individual had destroyed the children's library that was built beside our hut. The books had been generously donated by my friend's parents in England. This person had removed all the books, claiming we were promoting a Western lifestyle to the youth. Tragically, that same evening, this individual was fatally shot by the Nepal army, who were trying to maintain peace and security in the camp.

I questioned myself for leaving our home in Bhutan to be safe. The mere thought of having shouted TN Rizal's name back in 1990, a man who was now threatening my life, filled me with regret and sorrow. The fear of potential kidnapping had become so overwhelming that I could no longer send my children to school.

I was deeply convinced that we were being held captive in the camps when I discovered through the US embassy in May 2007 that TN Rizal and his team had scheduled a meeting with the American Ambassador to request the US government to withdraw the resettlement offer.

Nonetheless, Voice for Change successfully coordinated travel, and lodging arrangements for 17 members of the Durable Solutions Committee to convene in Kathmandu. Equipped with an appeal bearing 75,000 refugee signatures, the committee presented their petition for a durable solution to the US embassy, UNHCR office, Australian and Canadian consulates, and others.

In December 2007, I received a phone call urgently calling me to the International Organisation for Migration (IOM) office in Kathmandu. Upon arrival, I was met by officials from the US embassy and IOM, who advised me to keep a low profile for my safety. Subsequently, I was informed that a woman in the camp had overheard plans of a group of seven individuals from a Maoist political group heading to Kathmandu with the intent to harm me. This courageous individual promptly reported the threat to the UNHCR field office in Damak.

We underwent our pre-travel vaccinations in Kathmandu before receiving a call from IOM advising us to secure an exit permit from the Home Ministry Office, which would allow us to leave the country. However, upon our visit to the ministry, we were denied an audience. The following day, we were instructed to pack our belongings and report to the IOM office in Kathmandu. After a week-long stay at a hotel, we were flown to Jhapa district with an escort to obtain the necessary exit permit from the Nepal government.

On February 26th 2008, the day of our departure, as we arrived at the airport at 9 am for our 2 pm flight, I overheard UNHCR officials making multiple calls to convince the Nepal government officials to allow our "first case departure." Despite challenges with airport officials about recognizing our documents, the supportive IOM officials, stood by our side throughout the ordeal. By noon, the issues were resolved, allowing us to proceed. Before boarding the plane, the IOM officials requested that I send them a text message once we were on board so that they could leave the airport. We were the first Bhutanese refugees to be resettled to the US.

After 7 years in the US, we became American citizens. Still longing to return home for a visit, we applied for visas to visit Bhutan. Our visa applications were rejected and 25% of our hard-earned money was never returned. We are still longing to be able to at least visit our home in the future, but so far this has not been possible. We keep hoping for a time when our dreams of returning might come true.

Social Activist Versus Motherhood

Reportage by Haydeh Ravesh

A mother's love towards her children has often been described and admired as a unique relationship in human history. To be a mother entails joyful feelings and experiences that could facilitate social maturity and emotional development. Motherhood also involves new challenges that require patience, hard work and often daily unexpected problems. However, to be a mother and political activist simultaneously creates tensions anew. On the one hand one must attempt to be a conscientious mother who is aware of her responsibilities, and on the other live as a social activist who feels socially and morally duty-bound to participate in political activities.

I spent five years in Evin Prison in Iran[1]. During this time, I came across and lived alongside a number of women who were caught in between motherly love, and social engagement and public duty.

In the following, I present five narratives of such cases that show the complexity of decisions made by these women.

---

[1] Evin prison is located in North of Tehran, Capital of Iran, was built in 1970s. This prison detained mostly political prisoners and has earned a notorious reputation for Human Rights abuses and mistreatment of political prisoner.

1-Naaize

It was not a surprise that revolutionary guard came to arrest them. Because in the previous month multiple friends were arrested, mainly from their homes or workplaces, not randomly on the street. This indicates that the police guard must have had some information about their organisation.

At around seven in the evening, the house door buzzed for a while, someone's finger was holding the button down. The couple, both in their early 30s, looked at each other with widened eyes filled with fear. They had a toddler, an eighteen-month-old girl, Naaize. After they opened the door more than ten paasdaars[2] with guns poured into the house running to different rooms, upstairs, the kitchen, the bathroom – everywhere.

In the sitting room were two walls covered by bookshelves that caught attention of the paasdaars. The books were their university textbooks, the books and magazines belonged to the man who was a social issues researcher, and poems and fiction books which belonged to the woman.

---

[2] Paasdaars are members of Islamic Revolutionary Guard Crops, an ideological military service that established after Islamic Republic gain the power in Iran in 1979. They defend and protect the Islamic rules and values both internal and external of Iran

The paasdaars were angry at seeing such a big number of books. They started to throw them down off the shelves, trying to break off their covers and tear their pages.

Both the man and woman were standing in a corner of the sitting room motionless as they had been ordered to by the lead guard, who kept his gun pointed at them. But the little girl was walking around, and both parents were talking with her to pretend nothing was wrong and these guys were not harmful.

At some point the little girl stated to go to the books picking them up and putting them in a pile while saying to the guards: "The books are nice, we look after them, be careful they are delicate and cute!"

The head guard couldn't stand it. He stared to shout at the little girl and saying: "Shut up you little bastard. You are as nasty as your atheist parents." Then with a louder voice he shouted at the woman: "Pick up this child and make her quiet!"

At this point Naaize started to cry hysterically. Even being in her mother's arms didn't help her to calm down. She cried for a long time, eventually while she was still murmuring about the books, she fell asleep.

2-Aezam

After being held in Evin prison for over three years, Aezam was eventually released. She was the mother of two young girls; one was a toddler and the other one was almost three years old when Aezam was arrested. Aezam's husband was in another prison called Goohar-dasht and had an eight-year sentence.

Aezam went for the very first visit to the prison in a green dress, her husband's favourite colour. She, like all the other women visitors, had to wear a black chador – a piece of cloth covering her from head to toe. However, she would use some short minutes to open up her Chador to show her beloved husband the green dress. The visit, even behind a glass cabin and for only ten minutes, was still joyful after two years. They had another visit two weeks later, soon after that all visits were banned in all of Iran's political prisons. The rumours about massacres became stronger and after almost two months everybody knew that it was a sad truth, as opposed to harmless gossip. [3]

Aezam's father and her brother-in-law started to go to the prison door, prison office, and courts of justice to get any news about her husband. She was busy with their children and looking after her elderly mother. Anyhow, in Iran it was widely known that it would be much more effective if men go to these types of offices.

---

[3] 1988 Mass execution started in July 1988 and continued for about five months, a series of mass executions of political prisoners ordered by Ayatollah Khomeini, the killing took place across Iran, and The Amnesty International estimated 30,000 people killed.

More than one month went by living in hesitation and anxiety, being nervous and worried about the lack of news. In one afternoon Aezam was at home when her father and brother-in-law returned. They looked shattered and sadder than the previous times. They broke the news to Aezam that her husband, who was in his early 30s, had been executed by hanging. She burst into tears, shouting: "He was too young to get die; he had a sentence why did they kill him? Oh, I can't believe all we had was only two visits behind the glass barriers and that was all…"

The two men and her mother attempted to calm her down, which wasn't helpful at all. There were some noises in the garden and the entrance door opened Aezam's children were brought home from school by Aezam's younger sister.

Aezam face was covered in tears. As her children returned, she speedily ran behind a sofa and lay down on the floor. She wiped her tears, rubbed her cheeks and took a number of deep breaths.

Meanwhile the girls were asking about their mother, while Aezam's parents were asking them about what they would like for their afternoon snacks and avoiding answering them. As they didn't know why Aezam was lying behind the sofa.

After two or three minutes Aezam shouted: "It's hide and seek, can you find me!" The girls had a happy scream and moved towards the sofa. Aezam, with a big smile, came out and cuddled them tightly.

The rest of the evening went as usual, having snacks, watching TV, doing homework, dinner and then showering.

The girls shared a bedroom with two single beds in parallel on each side of the room a rug in between on the floor. Aezam usually lay down on it either to read to them books or to tell them stories every night.

That night she read a short book. When the children were about to sleep, she started to cry quietly.

The tears were relentless. They had built up over those hours that she stayed quiet and calm for her girls. Aezam cried and cried while she decided that she would have to cry quietly forever to avoid making her children sad and depressed, or full of bitterness at the injustice of their father's death.

The following day she contacted a child psychologist to seek advice about how to break this terrible news to these two little girls, who had only just had their freed mother back home for three months. Their mother had been missed for longer than three years during her imprisonment. Now they would have to face up to the loss of their father and never see him again.

3- Narges

Mother Narges (translates to Daffodil in English) was known at Evin prison. I had heard about her a couple of times during my time in there, but never had met her until my last year.

She was in her late 60s, of medium height, a bit chubby particularly her tummy. Her hair was completely grey, nice and shiny. She had small piercing black eyes and a mouth with narrow lips which always were smiling.

Mother Narges had a number of sons whom she brought up by herself. Her husband died very soon after the last boy was born.

Two of her younger sons were members of an Islamic revolutionary group. When they were at risk of arrest, mother Narges helped them to hide and eventually she helped and covered them to leave the country.

As the police were looking for them, they found out that the two young men had disappeared. They arrested the mother to get some information about them.

Mother Narges was so brave, strong and clever. She also looked quite calm and honest.

All this made it harder for the police to interrogate her and gain some clue about her sons' where abouts. However they beat her badly and broke one of her legs. After months being in pain and not receiving enough treatments, she couldn't bend her knee, and also sitting and standing up was difficult and quite painful even after a couple of years.

The police guards interrogated her for days, constantly asking questions, threatening her, patronising and beating her. But mother Narges stayed quiet. When they slowed down she told them: "How silly you are, how superficial and shallow. 'You think even if I knew where my children were, I would tell you? You do not know how I brought up them with difficulties; you do not have any understanding of motherhood and mothers' love. I think that you never received a deep love from your own mother. So you are expecting by beating and hurting my body I would betray my sons and would put them in danger. I would be happier to die from your tortures, than I get released and have one of my sons arrested."

They kept mother Narges in prison until the end of the big massacre in 1988(3). They eventually conditionally released her – that whenever they contact her she should go back to the prison office and if she gets any information about her sons she must immediately inform the police guards.

4- Parivash

In the prison all the women who had a child or children were called 'mother' to show respect to them.

Mother Parivash was in her late 30s tall and slim looked quite strong particularly when she walked fast in the prison garden. She was a well experienced GP; Parivash worked at hospitals in very deprived areas of Tehran – the capital of Iran.

Whenever one of us went to Parivash to talk about any health problems, she responded positively, listened very carefully and looked at that person with kindness in her eyes.

Once I had a bad backache, the doctor of prison gave me a cream to apply and some painkillers. Walking and sitting were so painful for me; even while I was lying down I still had pain. I talked about my problem with Parivash, she said: Your back has got a problem it takes weeks to get well. During this time medicine makes you better, exercise help you, your body will do some recovery and the other part is that anyhow you have to bear/tolerate the pain and be patient.

It was the very first time I was hearing from a doctor that I have to tolerate pain and also considering my body's ability for recovering and getting better, a different approach and attitude towards illness and being unwell.

When Parivash was arrested her only son was a 7/8-year-old. They had no relative to look after the young boy. Parivash's sister, who was single and lived in a city near Tehran, took the responsibility.

In order to avoid pressure on the child at school they decided to tell the school that her auntie is in prison and he gets off from school to visit her. On the other side he gradually called his auntie 'mother'.

Parivash was kept in prison for almost eight years. When she came out, she had no jobs and no big money. She visited her son and her sister so often but always felt a space with her son.

Parivash considered it due to the eight years distance and also he was a teenager. She thought time would help especially when they live together.

After months Parivash got a good job in a clinic with reasonable payment. Then she was able to afford renting a decent flat with enough space for her and her son.

When Parivash finished sorting out the rented flat with new furniture and decoration, she went to her sister's place to take her son. In her surprise he refused to leave there and join Parivash for living. He said that he had not received any love and care from her. But it was his auntie who had really been mothering him, so he wouldn't let her have to live alone.

Parivash tried to explain her situation and talked about her great love for him. Parivash sister kept silence in this conversation in a way to keep the son for herself. But the teenage boy did not change his mind and kept to his decision.

Parivash went back with broken hearted, felt lonely with a big loss over the years that she suffered in prison which not only hadn't brought any love or respect from her son but blaming and avoiding her.

Parivash carried on with her job and tried to concentrate on her job and get satisfaction from her patients' treatments. But it did not work well. After a while she committed suicide and died with a sad and broken heart.

5-Zoia

Zoia was just shy of twenty-four when she was arrested. In the prison ward, she was perpetually calm, well-mannered, respectful and quiet with all. It took about three years until the prison officers took her to court and after a number of weeks, she was informed about her sentence. It was quite common for prisoners to first be interrogated and kept in a cell, followed by being sent to the general ward, where they waited for further action or procedure for months or even years. These years would not be counted as part of the sentence. The sentence started from the date of issue. In this way a prisoner could end up imprisoned for five years, but would only be formally charged with a two years sentence. These years or months seemed like lost and wasted years in a prisoners' life.

When they called Zoia to go to the office to sign her sentence, for the very first time, I saw her destabilized by her anxiety. With jerky gestures, she put on her headscarf and black Chador.

Then while Zoia was twisting the straps of her blindfold[4] she looked over at me and two other friends standing near her, saying "Wish me a short sentence – less than ten years!" We gave her a hug and kissed her; we also tried to assure her that she wouldn't get a long sentence.

It was not longer than an hour before Zoia came back. Her face already appeared older and she had that familiar look of exhaustion, fear and disappointment that was so common in Evin. Taking off her chador and blindfold, Zoia sat down and held her head between her hands. Her eyes were resting on the ground only and she stayed quiet for a while.

We sat around her waiting in silence for her to talk and break the news. Zoia took a deep breath, lifted her head and said 'FIFTEEN YEARS!'

The energy was sucked out of the room, the silence became heavier. After a few seconds, with a dry smile Zoia said she was happy to have such good friends and kind roommates. Then Zoia added that she would try to stay hopeful that maybe they would reduce the sentence after some period of time.

After two or three days when Zoia and I were walking in the prison yard she started to talk. She said: "I don't mind being in prison for ten years or fifteen years, but I'm thinking of

---

[4] Blindfold was a relatively big strip of black cloth that all the prisoners had to put on their eyes whenever they leave their ward or their cell.

having a baby." Then she added: "If they keep me here for fifteen years, at the time of my release I will be almost forty years old, and by that point there's no chance of getting pregnant and having a child."

In between these words she started to cry and spoke with increasing despair. I held her hand and tried to calm her down. Zoia and so many more young women were kept in prison for such a long time that they passed the age of getting pregnant and having a child. Imprisonment can trigger innumerable subtle damages to prisoners and also to their families, which are not easily visible. Having lived and bonded with women like Zoia, her story is a reminder that life does not simply resume upon release. Rather the years taken from you serve as a punishment in themselves, and women can find their life trajectory permanently altered by the time that is so brutally snatched away.

Conclusion

Being a woman during Iran's Islamic Revolution, and in the years which followed was under no circumstances easy. An added pressure was faced by mothers who felt a duty to participate, engage in and lead political activism during an era of tumult and repression.

These mothers were subject to the restrictive government rules and control over their clothes, which were enforced with the blunt tools of authoritarian rule. Alongside this, mothers faced less opportunity in finding a job and came under greater risk of being sacked due to having a baby.

Iranian women, like many women who live under authoritarian Islamic regimes, have to fight the values in their family and also the social communities. A whole range of families, who align with more traditional, are against their daughters living as social or political activists. The judgment of families and friends who don't believe in the right of women, especially mothers, to be an activist is another pressure for these mothers.

These activist mothers are constantly in huge debates between pursuing their purpose and passion as political figures and staying committed to their children. Being caught between two powerful loves and responsibilities, and to nurture both of them in such a challenging climate, can be a great deal of pressure.

They have to stay calm and quiet and hold in their anger like Naazie's mother, and in other moments they have to hold in their tears and pretend to be happy like Aezam, or tolerate all the torture to save their children like Narges.

However, they all – through their respective strength and vulnerability – contributed more dignity and value to what is understood as "motherhood."

Love and Shame

Story by Nasrin Parvaz

One evening as Bahman turned into his road and looked up at their apartment window, he saw the red curtain was drawn, highlighted by the lights inside. He stood in front of the first house he reached and put his hand up near the bell. He watched the road to see if there were any cars and if they had noticed him. He saw a few cars near to their house and there was someone behind the wheel of one of them. Pretending no one was home, he turned away and left. No matter how many security guards were inside his parents' house, his mother managed to signal to him in the hopes it would warn him not to go inside.

As he walked away, his heart was with his parents who he knew were under interrogation. *Where can I go?* he thought. It wasn't safe to call his workmates. Instead, he called one of his friends from a public phone, whom Bahman thought might be the safest place for him. Arash wasn't politically active and wouldn't be under the regime's surveillance. As he dialled the number, he worried Arash might not be at home. His job was driving a lorry and sometimes he did not go home for days. As his friend answered the phone, he felt his spirits lift slightly.

"Hi Arash, I'm so sorry to ring late."

"It's fine Bahman. How are you?"

"I'm okay."

"You don't sound okay. What's up?"

"Well, I know it's late, but can I come over to stay with you for the night?"

"Of course, we're waiting for you."

He knew Arash from high school. While he went to work in a factory, Arash found solitary work as a lorry driver but he had always admired those who were struggling for their basic rights. Arash had gotten married two years ago and Bahman had gone to his wedding party. After that, he had visited them a few times and they had been to Bahman's parents' house. Bahman's parents liked Arash and his wife, Narges.

When he arrived, they had already made dinner for him and put it in front of him immediately, but he didn't have an appetite.

"I can't go home and I can't go to work tomorrow."

"Don't worry. You can stay here as long as you want."

"Can you call a friend of mine? I think he's safe, but I don't want to call him from your place, in case his number is bugged. Can you call him from a public phone? I'll tell you what to say."

"Sure."

"He can get me a forged birth certificate, so I can go to another town to live and work."

"Tell us what you were doing this time that the regime thought it was dangerous and arrested your workmates," Arash said.

"Well, all we want is a union in our workplace. A few workers were arrested and it seems like one of them couldn't bear the torture and mentioned me."

Two days later, they were listening to the news when they heard the usual announcement: "These individuals are dangerous and people should report them as soon as they see them."

They looked up to see the photos, when suddenly they saw Bahman's picture beside a few men on TV.

Bahman looked at his hosts, who, like him, were shocked.

"I'd better go. I might put your life in danger if I stay here."

"You don't have anywhere to go. Stay here, but I think you shouldn't go out. The neighbours might recognise you and report you," Arash said.

"Is it okay with you too?" Bahman asked Narges, who seemed terrified.

"Of course. How can they show pictures of people like you on TV and say you are dangerous?"

"We *are* dangerous. Not to the people though, to their system and their power."

"Instead of the prison they want to take you to, you have to live like a prisoner here," said Narges.

"My two weeks off work are nearly over," Arash told him. "The day after tomorrow, I'll hit the road again and won't come back for a week. Is there anything you would like me to buy for you before I go?"

"Yes, please. Buy some books for me to read. Now that they have my picture, I can't stay in the country. I have to leave it as soon as possible. I never liked going out of the country. What am I going to do in another country where I don't understand their language?"

Arash and Narges' place was a one-bedroom flat and Bahman had to sleep in the sitting room, where they all spent their time during the day. Days passed, while he was busy reading and Narges worked on her knitting machine. She gave him her husband's clothes to wear after his shower. At lunch time and dinner, they talked at length about each other's lives and how he became interested in politics. She knitted cloths for people and took them to their houses and collected money. He cooked and cleaned the house when she was out. She was surprised by this and told him he didn't need to do it.

"Why not? I cooked and cleaned my place. Why shouldn't I do it here?"

"Arash doesn't do these things. And I don't mind. His job is tiring and he needs to have a rest at home."

He didn't say anything, but he didn't agree with what she said. He saw that her work was tiring too.

Three weeks had passed and he had finished all the books Arash had bought for him. He realised Arash and Narges weren't book readers. During those days when he read something interesting, he asked her if she would like him to read it to her and she would say yes. Now that he had no new book to read, he re-read passages of them which he liked.

One day, when Narges was going out to buy some food, she asked him if he wanted anything.

"I'd like something. But I'm embarrassed about not being able to pay for it. I'm a burden on you two. I don't know how to pay back."

"Don't ever say that. I'm glad to know you. I wish you didn't have to leave us."

He noticed her blush. As if she thought out loud and hadn't meant to reveal it.

"I used to paint when I had time. Can you buy a sketchbook and some cheap water colours for me?"

Her eyes shone. "Of course. I'd like to learn how to paint. Perhaps I can learn to paint by watching you doing it."

"I can help you by showing you a few tricks. It's not difficult."

He watched how happy she became before going out of the house.

For a few days, he only painted anything he could see in the house: shoes, his hands, the flower vase, the chair, the table, etc. He painted his feet and his toes from different angles, thinking the pain they were going to endure soon walking in the mountains so he could cross the border.

Narges admired all his paintings and helped him to put them on the wall. She would sit beside him and imitate him by painting the way he did when she had no work to do. She wasn't happy with her painting, but he encouraged her and told her that she had to paint often to learn how to do it.

One day, when he had become bored of his surroundings, he said, "What can I paint?"

"Would you like to paint my face?" Narges asked.

"Yes, that would be nice, if you don't mind. I can paint you while you do your knitting."

She continued her work, but Bahman realised she had lost her natural way of sitting. In fact, she was posing and tried to move as little as she could while her hands moved over the machine.

By the time Arash came home for a few days, Bahman had painted Narges's face a few times. Arash was happy to see them. Bahman listened to the stories that Arash brought from other cities and the long roads he drove.

"I called your friend's number every day, but there was no reply."

"Thanks. He must be away. I'm sorry I've been stuck here and I'm a burden on you two."

"Don't ever say that again," Arash said, sounding offended.

While Arash was at home, Bahman painted a few portraits of him. Arash chose one and put it on the wall in their sitting room beside Narges's picture.

"Can I paint you again, while you're working?" he asked once again when he had nothing to read and Arash was away.

"Sure. You don't need to ask."

The next day she wore pretty clothes he had not seen her wearing before. It highlighted all her curves. While she was knitting, he painted her and fell in love with the woman in his sketchbook. He thought it couldn't be love really, it was just that he had not seen any woman for three months now and it was inevitable to fall in love with the only woman he was seeing. He decided he wouldn't let his feelings win over his reasoning. He would not touch her, even if he was in love with her. She was his friend's wife; Arash had saved him and he could not betray him. He looked at her face in his paintings. In some she was happy and excited as if she was dreaming of something extraordinary and he wondered what it was. In others she seemed sad, bored, thoughtful and frustrated.

The following day when he started to paint her, she unbuttoned her top and exposed her breast. Though he was sitting away from her, he could feel her heavy breathing. He thought trouble was coming. Had she fallen in love with him too? He tried to stay cool and painted her body from the side, not showing her bare breasts. As soon as he put down the brush, she left her knitting and came close to see her portrait. She seemed disappointed to see he had not painted her the way she had posed.

"I'm sorry. It's not as good as you expected," he said.

"There is nothing to be sorry for," she said. Then her hand touched his face and he found himself shaking slightly.

She went back to her machine and continued knitting. She was sad now, very sad and didn't look at him anymore. Her breast was still exposed. Bahman took his smaller sketch book and drew her face and body; her breast seemed to be trying to come out of the paper. He was thinking about Arash hitting the road, leaving him here with his young wife.

Taking a break, she looked at his sketches briefly. As time passed, her dress became looser and looser. Now she was doing her job naked and Bahman sketched her one after the other without feeling tired.

One late evening, he was reading a book when she said goodnight to him. He heard her getting ready and going to bed. He went to bed, thinking it could not continue like this and he had to go before anything happened between him and Narges. But how could he get away without help? He would get arrested if he used his name. Arash was away and wouldn't be able to come home for another two weeks. His mind was full of worries when he heard some soft footsteps. His blanket lifted and Narges moved inside. She was naked.

"I love you. You're different from all the men I've met before."

"Listen, Arash trusted us; we shouldn't do this."

'He doesn't need to know." She started to kiss him.

He'd never had such conflicting feelings. His body was craving to touch her, to kiss her and discover her body, while his mind was reasoning with him that it wasn't right. Soon, he realised they were locked to each other, crying. Her tears fell onto his lips and his tears, making her face wet.

For a few days, they could not let go of each other; their love was tense and he feared what would happen when Arash returned.

Arash came back and they both pretended that there was no secret between them. Every time Arash left for work, they soon made love, like two starved birds.

After five months had passed, he was reading a book and Narges was out, Arash came home from a few days' absence.

"I called your friend yesterday and this time he answered. I told him that you wanted him to take you to his brother's place. This was your code, wasn't it?"

"Yes. What did he say?" asked Bahman, feeling anxious.

"He said he can pick you up tomorrow night."

"Thank you." Bahman said, feeling lost. He felt deeply in love with Narges and at the same time, he felt ashamed of what he had done to Arash. His friend had given him his trust and Bahman had failed to keep it.

"But he didn't tell me where he's going to see you and what time. You told me not to give him my address."

"I know where he will pick me up and what time. If you can take me to the place, after that everything will be fine."

"So, this is the last night you're here and tomorrow is the last day we have you?" As Arash said these words, the door opened and Narges came in. She seemed have heard part of her husband's words.

"What's happening?" she asked. She knew this moment would come, but she seemed not to have prepared for it.

"Bahman is leaving us tomorrow night," Arash announced. Narges left for the kitchen before her husband could see her face. But Bahman caught a glimpse of it; she'd turned white.

That night she didn't sit with them and said she was tired; she went to bed early. The two men sat and talked, drinking the forbidden wine.

The next morning while Arash was having a shower, Narges tried to reason with him, "Don't go, please."

"I can't stay here for the rest of my life."

"Then take me with you. Please let me come."

"Impossible."

"I'll tell him. I'll explain to him." Her voice was trembling.

"No. I can't do this to him," Bahman insisted.

"I thought you loved me."

He looked at her with pleading eyes.

"What about me then?" she asked, her voice choking.

"I'm sorry."

Arash came into the room, and Narges continued to prepare lunch. Bahman was busy with looking at his paintings, which he was going to leave behind. He put the sketches of Narges's nude body in his pocket. She didn't need them and Arash didn't know about them. He glanced at Arash, who was watching him closely. He realised he couldn't look into his friend's eyes anymore.

"You'll let us know as soon as you get to a safe place, won't you?" Arash asked.

"Sure."

"Are you worried?"

"A bit but I know the guy. He's good and he can take me over the border, if nothing happens on the way."

That day passed slowly. Narges busied herself with her work, but Bahman was aware that she looked at him now and then, while the two men were talking.

As Arash walked towards his lorry to sit behind the wheel, Bahman hugged Narges to say goodbye.

"I'm glad you left something of yourself for me," she said, tears in her eyes.

"Yes, I have you in my sketches. And I left the sketches of my feet and hands for you."

"You left me more than that," she said.

"Yes. We have our love," he said.

She was holding his hands, "I'll keep it with me for the rest of my life. Good luck."

As he was walking for hours and hours, he reviewed the images of those five months with Narges in his mind. Then, at some point, he thought about her words again: "I'll keep it with me for the rest of my life."

After a few days of walking, while he constantly craved a hot shower and a soft bed to sleep in, near the border, a realisation hit him. During the last month, many mornings, he had heard Narges being sick in the bathroom. He had asked her if she was okay and every time she had said it was nothing. His mind was so busy with his escape, that he hadn't thought about it all properly. Was she pregnant? Why hadn't she told him? What else had she meant, if she wasn't carrying his baby? Was he going to be a father who would never see his child?

Then he remembered in his early time with them, he had asked Arash if they didn't want to have children. Arash had said they wanted them but it hadn't happened yet. Bahman had joked with his friend, "Perhaps you don't try hard." He felt a bitter taste of having cuckolded his friend. Near the border, he realised that it wasn't only his feet which were burning from blisters. His heart was exploding from pain of wanting Narges and his child she was carrying. His head too was exploding with shame – Arash had trusted him.

When he had passed the border and reached safety, he sat down and cried hard. He didn't know who he was crying for: his parents, his unborn child, Narges or Arash?

One of the two men who accompanied him to safety said, "It's over man. Now we'll have food, shower and someone will dress your feet."

He thought: yes, someone could dress his bloodied feet, but no one would be able to mend his wounded heart. He wondered at what point his parents would draw back the red curtain, knowing he wouldn't return.

Oracle

Memoir by Anba Jawi

So, this was London!

The city I never visited once in my daydreams. Where is my year seven classmate, now? She used to sit just behind my desk. She was kind, friendly and pleasant. I sat alone in the first seat, on the left side of the room. The rest of the class were in twos with a longer width than my desk. The few shorter inches forced the form teacher to offer it to one student and I was the lucky one. I preferred being alone, was shy. I was the only one who came to this secondary school from my primary school. My year six classmates went to the nearby school while I went further to a school near the state radio station. I did not have the courage to talk to any girl in the class. Ameera was sharing her desk with another girl and instead of talking to her she knocked on my shoulder, starting to chat to me as if she has known me for many years. We became friends; she was the only girl I talked to in the whole school. Ameera was cheerful and in the playground, we would walk together and chat. She took part in the school play, and managed to get the lead role while I failed even to be an extra. I am not sure if she liked me because I was top of the class. I never told her I like reading literature in case she might feel embarrassed. I gathered she did not read. Maybe she liked me because she saw inside this shy girl. She chose to be my friend because of her instinct. One day during a break between lessons, we stayed in the classroom because of heavy rain. She took a piece of paper and folded it into four pyramids. She smiled and said I am a paper cone gazer. Ameera looked into my eyes, moved her four fingers under the cone paper front, back, left, right reading my future.

"You will live in London and have two girls!"

The four protruding cones offered many cities and capitals. Paris, the city of Honore de Balzac, the Eiffel Tower and Brigitte Bardot films. Rome Oh Rome the dream city, Trevi Fountain, Italo Calvino and Sophia Loren. I was keen to see New York especially that huge fat lady named the Statue of Liberty and see Tiffany to find out why Audrey Hepburn ate her breakfast near the shop. But Ameera the fortune teller picked me up from the classroom and threw me in London; such is my luck, I suppose. London did not attract my attention. I knew about Tower Bridge and Trafalgar Square and Jane Austen and Richard Burton. It was not attractive enough for me, perhaps due to most Iraqis having crush on London. I didn't like to be part of the herd.

I thought I had escaped my fate.

Sixteen years later, involuntarily landed in London, I was worried. My mind was occupied by which lie I would use to pass through immigration. The number of people arriving from different destination formed a long queue which moved like a turtle. I could see people being questioned by the officers behind the desks. The scene scared me: if I messed up and showed I was lying it would be the end for me. My stomach started churning; *not now: I don't know where to go*. I felt cold and my legs became thin strings with no weight. Finally, I reached the desk, and I handed over my passport. The immigration officer looked at the passport and examined my face then looked again at the photo and asked the reason for my visit? Shopping, I said. He believed me. I remembered reading an article in a newspaper about Middle Eastern visitors conquering Oxford Street shops. He would not believe me if I said I would like to visit the British Museum to see the Mesopotamian section, and would love to see Nabu, God of Writing! The Babylonians worshiped him; Hermes is his Greek equivalent. I did not look like that sort of person, keen to visit museums. Shopping suited me better.

Now I was here, and Oh My God London was not clean! The narrow streets were not straight and if I took a wrong turn I would fall into a maze although I had my A to Z London, my bible. I could not do without it and even then, I usually got lost in this busy city. I got a headache from the noise; people were always in a hurry and very occupied, not aware about their surroundings, in a daze. They did not look at you, in a different zone. Or was it me? I had landed here from different planet.

The food was another story. On my first day, I made a mistake and ordered a big burger. It landed at my table, a tower, layers of meat and cheese and other things I never saw before. We eat one piece of meat back home the size of an egg. That would be my share from the saucepan my mum would cook for the whole family, in total ten people. I sat in front of this tower wondering, how I am going to eat this tower? Is this creature really my order, or has this landed on my table by mistake? My order resembled my landing in London. Unintended.

I went to UCL and visited the Micropaleontology department. The head of the department met me, Prof Barnard, I shook the hand of Alfred Hitchcock, disguised as head of department of a science subject. I told him about my experience working for seven years at the Iraqi Geological Survey at the Palaeontology department. His eyes lit up and smiled at me. He started asking specific questions only specialists in the subject can answer and I was more than happy to go into details. I love talking, like my grandmother; it is in the genes! Then I had to tell him, I did not have samples. He paused and looked at me. Usually, overseas PhD students come with samples from their own country to embark on a journey discovering the fossils of that area and the particular geological era. I was sitting in front of him empty-handed with my knowledge and experience as micropalaeontologist, and that was it. His blue eyes widened, looked me in the eyes and said, "have you escaped?" I laughed. That was my answer.

He said, "Okay, come on Monday to start. I will register you as one of my PhD students."

And that was it. I walked to Euston station thinking he really is Alfred Hitchcock. How did he know I fled my country?

The cone paper forecaster missed a small but major detail. She did not inform me about my arrival. I had to leave. Just to be safe, my family shipped me; they shipped the troublemaker, who spent her time meeting women's rights activists. It is interesting, throughout history, in all countries when the rulers attack women, it marks the beginning of a dictatorship. One can measure the level of civilisation and freedom in any society by looking at the plight of the women. My family made sure I left in time. Shortly after my departure, the authorities rounded up many I knew and worked with. My family were relieved they were quick to save me.

My plan was to stay in London for four years to finish my PhD. I thought that would be more than enough time for the situation to change back home. A country never stalls. There would be a military coup and I would go back to Baghdad. Life proved me wrong. I never went back.

Monday came and I was introduced to other postgraduate students, some home grown and some overseas. The first thing I asked them during the coffee break was whether they go to the cinema. They were surprised. Oh… they don't know, what it meant to me. To see a film in Baghdad I would have to ask many people and it would take days to organise. We would have to go as a group. If I could not find any one to go with me, I would gather my younger sisters and brothers, push them in a taxi like sardines in a can. No single girl would dare go to the cinema alone, that would be out of the question. In London, I learnt to go on my own and of course I chose to see the film My Fair Lady. I had read the play by George Bernard Shaw back home, a new copy. They showed the old film with added new shots omitted before, including the song "wouldn't it be loverly" by Audrey Hepburn in her own voice. I enjoyed it so tremendously that I saw it twice.

I couldn't believe how many theatres were in London. Never having seen a musical before, I wanted to see Evita and the opera Madam Butterfly was top on my list. Tickets were pricy. One day I thought I could with reducing expenses. Discovering mysterious London and immersing myself with study and preparing slides for the electronic microscope, I tried to keep busy and not occupied with what is happening back home. I struggled to sleep, and nightmares were a companion. News reached me. In Baghdad, some were taken to torture chambers and never came back. Some were forced to sign a pledge …some were poisoned … and some had various car accidents…

Walking alone around Camden market, drizzling, midday, Sunday it was. It was my kind of place, like the chaotic markets of Baghdad. My cup of tea as the English say. A student who was completing his thesis told me there are many terms describing the rain, maybe like in the Arabic language there are uncountable names for camel. I liked buying vegetables from the market; going to the supermarket gave me a headache. How many brands for butter or pickled cucumbers did I try? All have the same taste, far away from the pickled cucumbers back home. If they all taste the same what is the point of having shelves full of them? David Owen who was once foreign secretary and member of parliament for 26 years said in an interview, he could hardly find good apples in the shops. What? Did he shop in a supermarket? Had he seen the varieties there? I grew up knowing red and golden apples. They say it is matter of choice. Choice is an important word, the safeguard of liberty. I would like to see the right to choose something other than pickled gherkins though.

In London, my mind raced to grasp the various forms of entertainment on offer: Top of the Pops, Blankety Blank, Terry Wogan and Robin Day's Question Time. So many programmes! The shock was Janet Brown the comedian who impersonated Thatcher. Back home she would be killed a hundred times if she dared to make a joke about a prime minster let alone mimic him.

As for the Milk Snatcher, she was also named the Iron Lady. I preferred the first name. She should wear a Chanel suit to be true to herself. I was troubled by her tacky blue-coloured suits; she was Prime Minister (first woman prime minister in Britain) and should therefore be wealthy like prime ministers in the Arab world. They constantly stole public money. She should visit countries in the Middle East and see for herself. And as for that handbag, well it should be thrown in the bin. Her distasteful shade of blue is exactly same colour as the one worn by a peasant singer who appeared on Baghdad TV. A singer who could not sing and pretended he was brilliant. How did the English population vote for her? Did they have no style?

The Student's Union accommodation office arranged for me to live with an old lady as I requested, she lived in Camden Town with short distance to the tube station. I was happy, the room was large however the carpet had been there since the beginning of the universe. The heater ate my coins endlessly. I missed the oil burning slim heater back home, its place in the middle of the sitting room, the teapot on top of it marking the afternoon tea. The way we would sit around it, chatting about our day at school, events at work and how we would make stories as if we were inventing film titles like *fart in the middle of the ocean or screwdriver in the dark*. I could not believe my eyes when I saw the landlady immersing the dinner plates in soapy water in a bowl and took them out covered in the soap foam and arrange them in the plate drainer near the sink. What? we wash plates under running tap water. The thing that I could not adjust to was the bath. There was no shower, I was supposed to soak myself in a bathtub, not too bad but how I am going to wash my hair? I used to put the salad bowl in a carrier bag and take it with me to the bathroom and I used it to pour the water onto my hair to wash it then wash myself in that water afterward. I continued to wash myself like a dinner plate for more than a year. One day I forgot the salad bowl in my room. By that time, I start grasping the different accents and the way people spoke. Londoners hardly spoke proper English I thought. Regardless, London was my blanket, sheltered me, I felt safe and I liked how tolerant people were. I was ready to move.

I clutched the Evening Standard newspaper; after ensuring I had bought it at noon to catch any suitable "room to let" before they evaporated through the fog of this city. I looked through the price list and found an affordable, room, £9 a week in N16. Moving from NW1 to N16 did not seem significant. I took a few coins from my purse into my hands, strolled to the nearest available red telephone box and dialled the number for the N16 room.

"Aloo," I said.

"Good evening, young lady," he answered.

I moved back towards the heavy metal framed glass wall of the small red box. How did he realise I was young? The voice perhaps? He continued, "are you phoning regarding the room?"

"Yes sir. Can I come and see it?"

"Yes, yes do, I will give you the address, do you have pen and paper?"

I was struggling to understand his accent, his Rs were non-existent and it was as though he swallowed some letters. It occurred to me, why don't Londoners speak English?

"I will give you the address it's 71 Stoke Newington Church Street, N16."

"What?"

"S for Sierra, T for Tango, O for Oscar, K for Kilo, E for Echo …" He showered me with words, rapidly and without mercy.

"Mister, mister please!" The coins ran out and the phone line cut off.

I was bemused; why did this man live in a street which forces you to catch your breath after uttering it? Why didn't this man live on Baker Street or Bond Street or Oval Street where I lived or even Gower Street the precise place where I was standing using the red telephone box? Do affordable places deliberately have lengthy names to add value to them? How odd.

I pulled the heavy red door of the telephone box and exited humming the tune from the film "My Fair Lady:

Oh, why can't the English

Why can't the English

Learn to speak?

The Calligraphy Class

Novel extract by Sharif Gemie

Context: *It's September 1956. Nasser has nationalized the Suez Canal, igniting political and ethnic tensions in Britain, but there's no crisis yet. Nafah is a forty-one-year-old Palestinian refugee, living in London. Her British husband, Edmund, has left for Wales and she doesn't know when he'll return.*

I knew what to do: just like last year, get the fat book that listed all the classes, then choose one which wasn't too far away. I flicked through entries on architecture, Milton, philosophy for beginners and then saw a calligraphy class. The summary said you could change the sense of a word by writing it in a different style. Intriguing! Back in Jerusalem I'd studied calligraphy and no such promises had been made.

I felt awkward going by myself. Would I be sitting alone in the classroom? I could always leave, if I didn't like it. On Wednesday evening, I queued up to register with the familiar crowd of ladies, all anxious to improve themselves. I'd heard their chatter before: they spoke of their children's progress at school, their husbands' promotions and—in whispers—of other evening classes which might be better. I stopped listening and instead thought of decorated pages of the Qu'ran I'd seen in Jerusalem, with beautiful, flowing letters and borders decorated with flowers and leaves. I sighed. I wouldn't do anything like that here, would I?

A large lady came through the door. I recognised her, Gertrude Harris, from Edmund's bookshop.

'Ah, there you are,' she said. 'Now, what was your name?'

'Nafah.'

She frowned, thought for a moment, then looked straight at me.

'How about Nancy? That'll be easier for both of us.'

I wanted to shout at her that Nafah was two simple syllables and it was impossible for a woman of even moderate intelligence to get it wrong, but someone tugged at my elbow.

'Hallo? Mrs Jenkins?'

I turned round. It was the tall girl from Edmund's jazz concerts, the one who did the Indian dances.

'May I?' she said and then stood next to me in the queue.

I struggled to remember her name.

'You're—you're...'

'Luna.' She offered me her hand.

'Nafah.' I pronounced my name as clearly as I could. I saw the frown, the famous frown.

'Na-fah,' she repeated slowly and smiled.

We found a desk at the back of a drab, dingy room. On the walls were a faded, creased chart of the kings and queens of England, a poster illustrating English folk dances and another poster of French irregular verbs. I stared at the dances. They looked silly, but I could see that might be fun.

One lady put her hand up to ask a question.

'Ah, Mr Watkins—' she began.

'Call me Mike.'

The ladies weren't at all sure about that. I saw them swapping glances. I remembered that Mike was one of Edmund's jazz friends. Maybe all that improvisation and free expression had inspired his approach to teaching. Or maybe he wasn't a proper teacher.

Mike was a short, tubby man, who smiled a lot and constantly corrected himself. For this first class, there'd be no practical exercises. Instead, he showed slides of calligraphy from the past: the Book of Kells, a Gothic Bible, William Morris's Kelmscott font, a Victorian greeting-card and a wartime poster of Mr Carrott telling people to eat healthily. With each example, Mike commented on how the letters were shaped and how they changed the sense of the words, pointing out details we hadn't noticed. He promised us that in ten weeks, we'd each be able to write in at least five different scripts. A buzz of anticipation went round the class. Then he handed out a list of materials to buy: three types of calligraphy pens, good quality writing paper and—if we wanted—a couple of writing guides.

In the interval, Luna and I went for tea together.

'Arabic,' she said. 'Isn't that different? Don't they write from right to left?'

'Very different.'

'Are you doing calligraphy to help you write English?'

'I've given up trying to do that,' I laughed. 'Edmund can read my writing, that's enough. I just want to try something new. But what about you? What attracted you to this class?'

Luna launched into a complicated explanation. She thought that words connected us to the ancient past and she wanted to… After that I got lost.

'Your dancing,' I said. 'At the jazz concert. Where did you learn to do that?'

Luna grinned. 'I just do it to annoy them. All that jiving gets so boring.'

'But the way you dance: it's Indian—I recognised the movements.'

'Is it?' she shrugged. 'It just seemed right for the music.'

'Are you still at art college?'

She wrinkled her nose, frowned. 'Not really. They were trying to prepare us for commercial work, so...'

'And now you...'

'A bit of this, a bit of that. You know.'

I shook my head. I had no idea what she was talking about.

Three weeks later, Mike set us a difficult piece of homework. This time, we were to pick a saying, any saying, and then illustrate it with a suitable design and font, all by ourselves.

'No more spoon-feeding!' he smiled.

Luna nudged me and whispered that three-quarters of the ladies would choose 'Home Sweet Home.' I laughed and whispered back:

'At least it's simple: just three words.'

I wondered what Luna would choose.

By Tuesday evening, I hadn't done Mike's homework. I needed to think of something quickly.

I sat in the sitting-room and, out of nowhere, I remembered a saying from my childhood: 'Love alone cuts arguments short.' That would do. I'd illustrate it with a bold, curving script, one which showed the force of the saying but which retained a sense of grace. I put one of Edmund's new LPs on the radiogram—not that clumsy, childlike jazz he liked, but Glenn Gould playing Bach, very fast and very delicately. I'd liked it as soon as Edmund played it. He wasn't so sure.

I let those delicate piano notes fly over me and used a pencil to sketch in bold letters with little decorative curlicues and dashes to balance them and suggest gentleness. Then I went over it again with a pen, only using black ink: no colours, for the text as a whole had to be simple and elegant, with clear curves, and I didn't have time to think of colours. I worked slowly, thinking about the proportions and overall shape of the text, taking care not to smudge it. By ten o'clock, I felt I'd finished. I stood the paper at the end of the table, up against the wall, and I stepped back to look at it. Not bad. I'd learnt something in Mike's class.

I studied it again, making sure that the text as a whole was balanced, vertically and horizontally, and then it hit me. What an idiot I'd been! What would Mike say? And the ladies? My text was in Arabic, not English. There was no time for another design.

The ladies queued at the door, each with a folder under her arm. I joined them, weighed down by the thought that I'd brought Arabic words, words from The Enemy, with me. Luna was late, as usual. She dashed in after I'd sat down and grinned.

'What saying did you choose?' she whispered.

'"Love alone cuts arguments short."'

She raised her eyebrows. 'Really!'

'What about you?' I asked.

'"Writing is like jazz. It can be learnt, but it can't be taught."'

I laughed. 'I like that, but I'm not sure what Mike will think. Isn't he trying to teach us writing?'

Luna shrugged.

'Who said it?' I asked.

'Some jazz musician.'

'Mike'll probably like it then.'

We giggled.

'Who said yours?' asked Luna.

'Some Muslim mystic.' I deliberately imitated her casual tone.

She grinned.

Mike walked in, took off his old tweed jacket, pulled out papers and books from his case, then looked at us.

'Well, tonight it's my turn to rest and your turn to do the work.'

Appreciative grins spread round the class. He really was a good teacher, he always got on our good side.

He pushed a desk to one wall of classroom.

'Can you all see this? We'll display your offerings here, one by one. Cynthia…'

A smartly-dressed blonde lady jumped at the sound of her name. She immediately looked embarrassed.

'No, why don't you start with—'

'We'll start with you, because yours will wake us up and set the standard.'

There was laughter all around the class and, after a moment, Cynthia joined in. Mike wasn't malicious and no one wanted to go first.

Cynthia had chosen a quote from the Bible: 'The things that are impossible with men are possible with God.' She used a Gothic script. Mike looked at her.

'This test—this test, well, it was so difficult, Mr Watkins, so difficult that it seemed impossible, and then I thought…'

Mike nodded and complimented her on the clean lines of her script and the balanced proportion of the design. Cynthia looked confused. I think she'd expected Mike to comment on her religious faith.

As the class progressed, I grew interested in what these ladies had chosen. It was like a short course in British culture. Several had searched in the Bible. There was 'For what shall it profit a man, if he shall gain the whole world and lose his soul?'. Shakespeare, of course. 'We are such stuff as dreams are made on.' 'To thine own self be true.' Beth Lewis surprised us with 'Plus ça change, plus c'est le même chose.'

'What does that mean?' Luna whispered to me.

'The more things change, the more they stay the same.'

Luna stared at me. 'What language is it?'

'French.'

Luna's guess about the ladies' choices was only correct in two cases: Jacqueline and Leslie had done 'Home Sweet Home'. To be fair, their designs were bright and cheerful. Valerie Henderson shocked us: 'From each according to his ability, to each according to his needs.' When she told us it was from Marx, there was complete silence. Then she spoilt the effect by adding:

'I was stuck and my husband told me to do that one.'

Were they Reds? She seemed such a polite, modest woman.

Mike complimented her on the round, regular script she'd used.

Luna's design was wonderful: a jumble of different scripts in bold colours, with the important words, jazz, writing and taught, standing out in bigger, clearer letters. I saw what she'd done: her design was like a jazz improvisation, with each of the different fonts contributing to the overall design.

Then it was my turn. I kept my design close to me as I walked to the display desk, not wanting anyone to see it too soon. I set it in place, then turned to face the class.

Frowns, perplexed frowns everywhere. Someone tutted.

'Is that writing?' muttered a lady at the back.

'Lovely script, beautiful letters,' said Mike, maybe a bit too loudly. He stepped closer. 'Nicely proportioned, too. Look at the balance of the letters.' He ran his finger along one line. 'So this is Arabic?' He looked at me and I nodded. 'Quite new to me. But what does it mean?'

'Love alone cuts arguments short.'

'Ha!' Mike laughed for a moment. 'Well, I certainly hope that's true. We could do with some of that at the moment.'

His words changed the tone in the classroom. Several of the ladies laughed with him, happily, not spitefully.

'But she hasn't written in English!' protested Gertrude Harris.

'Doesn't matter,' said Mike. 'Calligraphy's calligraphy, whatever the language.'

'That's not a script you taught us.'

Mike pointed at Luna's design. 'Calligraphy's learnt, not taught.'

After the class, Luna and I caught the bus to the high street. I glanced at the neat shopfronts and little brick walls and realised they formed a set of clear lines, curving along the road. Why had I never noticed that before?

I thought about my design and the reactions of the class. I felt happy, but something else as well—vulnerable, or worried. It had been interesting watching the ladies and seeing their choices. I remembered Mike's cheerful words, and said them over and over in mind. That had been good of him, but I couldn't rely on always having someone like Mike to help me.

'I won't do another piece in Arabic,' I told Luna.

'Why not?'

'It was a mistake—no one else in the room could understand it.'

'You heard Mike—letters express something, even if we don't know what they mean.'

I shook my head.

Mike had given me something important, almost like a new way of speaking. It had been a moment when I didn't have to pretend I was British or hide who I was. It was an odd feeling, almost like walking along the high street naked. I wasn't sure if I liked it. All this honesty was exhausting. I decided that my next design would be from Shakespeare. And I'd keep watching the ladies.

The Farmer's Daughter

Family history by Gilbert Luther

Late evening, late November in Moscow: snow, trodden and dog excrement-stained, leading to tall concrete blocks of flats rising clear of leafless poplar trees.

Temperature about minus twenty and falling: too bloody cold to be outside, stamping feet by a trolley bus stop, but the poor soul needed someone to ease her across the gap between bus and icy pavement even if the Bus Company have scattered cinders everywhere.

Helena has told me very little about her mother, Anna: "She'll probably be the only one getting off the bus at that hour and I've told her what you look like. Don't worry about it, she'll spot you and be so grateful for a steadying arm on this wretched ice. I bet her cronies know all about it."

All this in French of course: my Russian is very scrappy, and Helena knew almost no English when I met her back in spring, back in dear, old, little old, distant old England.

Her job, lecturing on economics to young aircraft technicians, keeps her very busy, while I have all the time in the world on my retired shoulders. And she has that growing lad to look after as well. Lucky her old mother can help with him.

Gradually I'm building a picture of the old lady's survival down to the present. Based on scraps of information, I make her about 68, in other words she would have been born about 1923.

I've been interested in that vast country, now called the Russian Federation, ever since I was at university (four decades ago) and finally came here with a host of qualms about the natives' probable attitude to me, a western capitalist. "What could he want with us? "The answer I suppose was easy enough to see 'cherchez la femme' as the French would say: whatever the problem, a woman is often the cause. Well, there was safety in that, wasn't there? And here I was picking up the woman's mother in classic Russian winter weather: a stout little bundle wrapped entirely in genuine fur - of what creature(s) I had little idea.

Such was my introduction to Anna. Very gradually I assembled the pieces that built her story, but even she can only surmise what really happened to that orphaned infant launched into such an unkind infancy.

Look for the Tyrant of course and this one had a power rivalling Genghis Khan's. There is no disputing his mental powers compared with those of normal men; no disputing his singleness of purpose; his swift perception of solutions to problems he spotted before his compatriots except for that time in 1941 when Adolf Hitler's generals appeared close to the very gates of Moscow with panzer divisions and an enormous hunger for oil. As a girl of eighteen, Anna had served tea to infantry soldiers already in their dug-out positions, though not all had a rifle.

Eighteen years before all that, Josef Stalin had a domestic problem — those wretched independent farmers who could hinder his plans for a revolution in agriculture: the solution, seizure by the State of all farms privately owned prior to collectivisation. The method was obvious: vilify the independent farmers with an appropriate label, "Kulaks" (the tight-fisted ones) and hound them into non-existence.

So off they were packed, on foot, 'escorted' in a north easterly direction, 'generously' allowed to take all they could carry in the way of tools, plus those members of the family too young or too old to walk.

For Anna, the little baby of one couple, you might well have thought this was the beginning of a very short existence. Indeed, within a couple of years she became an orphaned toddler in the care of others whose lives had also been violently disrupted. At least someone was found to 'look after' the little girl: though 'look after' hides the ironic reality of the carer being a blind woman.

Orphaned toddlers in her situation may be excused the pudding of recollections which they mix and carry with them, of those earliest years: when articulated they sound credible enough. Perhaps they have a need to push some of the actual ingredients right out of their memories and retain others which perhaps did not happen but make a soothing ointment of dreams.

Right from our first meeting however the old lady's mental fortitude was apparent and bound up with a strength of upper body anyone would have detected if they had escorted that stout little bundle of fur from trolley bus stop to her few rooms in one of those towering concrete blocks on that arctic night I first met her in Moscow. Those strengths, I surmise, must have been the one legacy her farming mother and father were able to leave with her: a resolute will in a body which coped with most loads it was obliged to hump between here and there: potatoes, swedes, millet and rye - when you were in luck - firewood. As for the ailments which winters inflicted and the lack of medicines, she had her share and her body remembered, as bodies do in old age.

She had grown into a handsome young woman and deserved better than her first suitor, father of her two girls, who was unfaithful even as she lay with her second baby in hospital. True to her nature, she made no compromises with him afterwards and knew how best to guard her babies' interests.

WW2 came to an end and a recently demobbed colonel of engineers met her. The rapport between him and this handsome young woman with two little girls blossomed into a firm and lasting attachment for the sixteen most formative years of the girls' lives, when the colonel died suddenly of a heart condition made worse by a war wound. His record as a builder of bridges on the battlefield, often under enemy fire, seemed like a symbol of his character — truly, fundamentally reliable.

He seemed to Anna like a divine recompense for her hazardous deprived childhood. He had never really spoken of his own childhood which, judging from his rank, record and age must have been very different from hers, even if marked by personal tragedy and battle fields.

Together, they had reared the two girls and seen they had the best education: at the French School in Moscow where both were prepared for university.

So, the colonel lived just long enough to see his stepdaughters launched into a post-Stalin world, and Anna, his youngish wife, their mother, in a position of being able to cope. She had never been a signed-up member of the Party but knew that her daughters from their beginning had no realistic future outside of the Party.

So how did Anna, the farmer's daughter, once again the only real support of herself but always with a mother's eye on her daughters and their children, continue to cope with day-to-day existence and its ups and downs?

The short answer to that is she knew her strengths, she had friends she had helped, and as important as anything she was prepared to rough it, by which I mean if there was a daily job in which you sat on a wooden box on a concrete floor in the entrance of the Moscow metro, selling carnets of passenger tickets in all weathers and then delivering the takings regularly and correctly to the transport offices then she was your 'man'. All of this in Moscow winters or summers, darkness or daylight, dangerous places, the usual crooks to look out for. The fact that she had a good fur coat and boots for the cold was an asset. Another asset was her money-counting skills, with or without her faithful abacus which, nightly, she plied, sitting on her sofa in her apartment.

How do I know all these details? Well, I lived with her and her elder daughter Helena for several months: autumn, winter, spring, before taking her daughter Helena off to England, where our son was born, reared and educated.

Anna was an example of so many in her own country, unhoused, unparented, deprived of all possessions, but she was not one of the thousands who quit Russia and went West with a few sovereigns sewn into their belts, the traditional refugees.

She had the nous to create a niche into which she fitted like a glove after the good fortune of having those vital years with the Colonel of Engineers. And I think you'd agree she had some luck in addition to her good looks – her marvellous head for figures, and her ability to spot a real bargain. Of all her accomplishments, that striving for the nurture and future of her own two daughters, Helena and Natalia, most impressed me. You might also agree with me that she made a sort of proxy emigration in the shape of Helena who was bearing our child when she came with me to England, leaving her mother behind.

You will understand me better if you could see this photo of an old lady proudly pushing a pram along the street of a provincial English town. She has a shawl round her head and is obviously well capable of the care in her hands: the little lad we called Sasha who had a beautiful smile and was a sturdy little fellow.

So, she had accomplished all she could and here was the icing on the cake. The farmer's daughter had seen it through as far as any woman could.

Sitting on the plane back to Moscow, she was at ease with herself as she saw, far below, that they were now flying over land clothed with dark green conifers. In little more than a month that dark green would mostly be white, as Napoleon once saw.

She had to smile at the quirkiness of fate, though not from thinking about Napoleon. Those raised on the land learn to live with the seasons and whatever comes over the horizon.

Her Two Scars

Short story by Marsha Glenn

Faye switches on the needle.

I'm going to start now. Are you ready, sweet pea? –

Sonchi stops breathing. Is she really ready for this? Does she have the strength to relive the horror, which will reach up from her memory when the needle hits the skin? Isn't it only safe to keep all that hurt in a trunk, locked up safely in her mind?

Here we go –

Sonchi follows Faye's serene voice, with its Australian twang. Lying on her back she can't see Faye or anyone else in the tattoo salon. She fixes her eyes on the intensely goth, tattoo-covered ceiling. Someone comes in, and the brass bell tinkles hastily, and loudly. It startles Sonchi who is already feeling vulnerable. She tenses her muscles unconsciously. Faye immediately stops the needle and strokes her ankle without saying anything. Sonchi pleads under her panting murmur:

Do not stop Faye. Keep your piercing weapon running onto me. –

She described the trunk to her therapist a few years back. In her mind, she pictured the trunk as a pirate treasure chest. This is where she kept all her trauma. Sonchi remembers when her therapist, professionally calm, asked specifically why the trunk was ornamented with shiny gems. She couldn't explain. Now she thinks, it was a desperate attempt to utterly deny the existence of those stacked-up memories. At the end of their time together, Sonchi deliberately left that invisible trunk in that therapy session room. Even now, she can see it in the corner behind the door, untouched in plain sight. She doesn't carry the cursed trunk with her anymore. But she still asks herself: what if she forgot to secure a lock on it? Then she might return to the time when she did not know how to pack all the sensory associations in that trunk along with the memories. The time when the feelings ambushed her successfully, triggering the memories of being interrogated, blindfolded car rides in the dark, and an avalanche of sadness in her heart.

Sonchi closes her eyes and works on her breathing to get herself in a relaxed mood. She knows the drill, it's time to practice her mindfulness lessons. She concentrates on the distant sounds, outside of the four walls she is in right now. People are laughing, someone is talking loudly on his phone and a young voice is asking questions without waiting for an answer. She is ready to imagine further away, where the Pacific Ocean claims its territory, and a sandy, remote beach, and rhythmic waves calling.

The jingling brass bell brings Sonchi back from the ocean shore. She tries harder to go with the flow. Now she starts to guess who is coming in through the door. It was one of her favourite lonely childhood games. Whatever hint the door gives away: the noise and force of the bell, the creak of the door or some other quality she might notice. The salon staff are quiet and quick when getting in and out during their frequent 'smoko.' New customers are hesitant and gentle pushers. And underaged enquirers slam the door hard on exiting, expressing their temporary frustration. Sonchi keeps her eyes closed and lets her brain do absolutely anything to keep from reaching back into the dark memory lane.

Faye is working in silence. Sonchi has a lot to take care of inside her head. She is neither interested nor capable of bonding with Faye over common interests like holiday destinations and celebrity gossip etc. She is rather comfortable with professional and transactional human interactions.

Faye's needle touches and pierces her dreary skin. The needle goes up and down, then down and up, goes round and round, filling up the void with night-dark ink. Faye whispers:

Sonchi, breathe and relax please. We need your blood vessels to be wide open -

Sorry –

Sonchi starts breathing in and out slowly again like she has learnt to do whenever she has panic attacks. Her nerve fibres pass the signals of pain to her brainstem. They come right back to her, making her leg twitch uncontrollably. As Faye wipes her skin, there is a soothing touch of dampness which replaces that stinging needle briefly. Sonchi wants to feel completely numb so as not to get startled by any physical sensations at all. It's embarrassing for her because she knows how overly sensitive she is! And lately, she hasn't experienced any kind of physical interaction so she is extra awkward about it. Sonchi has been religious about the two-meter social distance since the pandemic and prefers no one invading her personal space. Then she proactively blocks any possibilities of intimacy. For a while, this feels safe but then it is a whole world of loneliness. In the same way, she is alone now, getting this tattoo, no one to seek comfort from. Deep down she wants to hold Faye's hand, touch her to feel better. Instead, she lays there longing for a companion, desperately soaking-in Faye's spoken words.

Sonchi met Faye the day before during her free consultation session for half an hour. It was her first time inside a tattoo salon. She was anxious and nervous thinking about her first tattoo experience. She was relieved to meet the female artist. She has been surprised at her own bravery so far: not only deciding to have a tattoo, but planning the design, doing online research, booking appointments, and finally showing up at the salon doorsteps. But she couldn't think of another man causing her physical pain and damaging her skin. Faye had mentioned that getting ink is very addictive. Then she proudly displayed her fully tattooed arms. Other than those tattoos, Sonchi didn't see any other scar on her pale-yellow skin.

Sonchi wanted to have a tattoo on the top of her left hand.

I want to imagine my scar becoming a sea turtle and it swims away, leaving my body free –

Faye did not agree to the sea turtle. She warned Sonchi over and over that, as a first-timer, she wouldn't cope with the pain of a tattoo in that spot. But pain doesn't mean anything to her. She is more frightened of memories.

You don't know my tolerance of pain, Sonchi thought, my physical and mental pain, the pain of remembering the past, the pain of not having a future, the pain of deciding to disappear from the face of the earth, the pain of not trusting anyone, the pain of being alive, the pain of freedom, the pain of waking up from nightmares, the pain of been examined to prove what I had been through and the pain of thinking now and then no one will notice for a while if I drop dead tomorrow…

You told me no drugs or alcohol at least 48 hours before going under the needle. Only if you knew, losing my consciousness is how I deal with my pain. Pain doesn't finish with the sacrifices we make or once we get rescued…

Sonchi dives further down memory lane, bound to reconcile something long overdue, blending two different stories of her two scars. She is moving through sticky cobwebs of flashback. Sonchi consoles herself:

Ten years apart – I am swapping one of my worst memories. I am getting another scar, damaging my so-called temple. This time I know who is touching me, and I am ready to endure the pain. I need the pain to overpower the last one, which was done by a faceless nobody.

I got a second chance in life and I would do everything to heal my damaged soul. I will treasure my scars, new or old and embrace the physical and emotional pain with satisfaction. Look at me now, how far I have come along, I conceive my own scar and the tattooist gives it colour, shade and energy.

Now Sonchi has two Dandelion stems over her left ankle, one is fully bloomed and the other one losing pappus in the air. Maybe it is a cliché, but Sonchi knows this is what she wants to wear, a scar on her skin she now owns.

Every Black Rock

Memoir by dima mekdad

"Today I'm taking you on a two-in-one tour!" Dad announces. "First, I'm going to take you to the new city, to places I believe are of historic importance. Then, we tour the old city."

I sit in the car seat next to him, watching the dark blue sky lightening up slowly. It is five to seven in the morning. The sun has only just risen and we are heading out without having had breakfast.

"In my opinion, this building should become a museum." Dad stops the car by an abandoned building with no signage. Instead of asking him why, I make a comment about the big pond in front of it.

"So, you don't want to know why I think this building should be a museum?"

I smile. If we were in London chatting as we do on our evenings when he visits, I would have teased him further and postponed the question until later. But given it is a special tour, I ask rather reluctantly.

"*Hat lashouf, lesh?* Go ahead then tell me why?!"

Equally, Dad would usually join in the teasing and not answer. But today time is of the essence.

"Because this is the first electricity plant in Bosra. In the early 1940s, the wise old men decided to bring electricity to the homes of Bosra. They refused to sit waiting on the government of that time to do it. They collected money from all families and built the first electrical station in the region. It was at a time when the central cities of the governances did not have electricity, not Daraa, Sweida and maybe not even Hama. I think only Damascus and the big cities had electricity in homes at that time." Dad tells me the story with so much pride. He always has a special proud face when it comes to Bosra.

"Impressive!" I answer. We discuss what happened over the years, and why the people of Bosra today are not as strategic and forward thinking as they used to be in the forties and fifties. But the conversation turns bleak rather quickly. We change the subject.

Dad is driving while I sit in the passenger seat, playing tourist. As he drives, Dad tells me stories about nearly everything we pass. We get out of the car every now and then to take a closer look. When we arrive at the old city, we continue our tour on foot. Despite climbing up and down the rocks, my not-very-active father manages to play guide very well. His stories span over thousands of years.

"I had forgotten how warm autumn is at home, Dad. In London, I would need to wear a jacket to walk on an early morning in October," I tell him as we walk.

"Of course, London is way too cold. That's why my visits to you in winter are very short," he says, smiling proudly again. It is as if the warm weather of Syria was his own making. Dad enjoys it whenever London loses points against Damascus or Bosra.

Growing up, I used to visit Bosra, Dad's hometown, every other weekend with my family. Dad would drive us all an hour and a half south from Damascus. We'd spend the weekend at my grandparents' home. We used to get very spoilt by my grandmother's generous hospitality. My grandfather, uncles, aunts and cousins always showered us with so much love too. Bosra was the place where there was joy, fun and never any drama. It always felt like a mini holiday. Here I am, finally visiting again for the first time in over eight years.

Under the clear blue sky hugged by the sun rays, with my father and the black basalt rocks of Bosra, I'm listening to the stories. Dad is as good, if not better, a storyteller than I recall him as a child. Maybe as an adult I now know how to listen better. Maybe as an exile I have learnt to appreciate stories of home more.

"This church was built by the Byzantines in the early sixth century AD and it is also *dar Aami*, my uncle's home." Standing in the middle of an ancient church, he tells me all about the architecture of the building and how the Byzantine architects skilfully erected the arches of the heavy black basalt rocks. He then moves on to tell me how his uncle, whom I vaguely remember from my childhood, lived with his family in this church for many years.

"My cousins and I used to play here in this yard. There, under the staircase, was my secret hiding spot in hide and seek games. I always won!" He points at the crumbling-basalt-rocks staircase, then to where the kitchen and bedrooms used to be. There is a precious joy that shows on adults' faces, as they recall their playful childhood memories. I am grateful to witness it on my father's face as he tells his story.

Dad had told me many times before, that one of the things that made Bosra unique, is that its people lived in the old city over centuries until recent history. Some of the ancient buildings were inhabited until the war broke out at the end of 2012. As if hearing it for the first time, this piece of familiar information lands on me as a soft surprise.

From time to time during the trip, Dad tells me both the story of an ancient building followed by a modern story from his childhood or teenage years and the people who lived in those places. Like knitting a scarf of different colours, my father weaves the ancient history stories with contemporary ones. Like a child excited to know if the hero will win the battle, I cling to his every word.

Occasionally, I see new metal frames installed in windows or old white paint on some walls. I feel upset to see such ancient buildings abused. However, most of all, I feel in awe of the old city of Bosra all over again. I admire the buildings, for they not only stood tall for thousands of years, but also housed the lives of so many people — my own family members, my father — one civilisation at a time throughout history.

"Here we are at the Roman Mile. You can think of this street as Shaalan or Salhieh are for modern day Damascus. *Ya'ani*, even like Oxford Street in London. It used to be the centre of all shopping and socialising activities in the ancient Roman Bosra."

In the centre of the old city, the Roman Mile divided the city to north and south sides, just like the river Thames divides London. The mile-long street starts and ends with triumphal arches. It was cobbled in the Roman times. Once there used to be shops, baths and full lives here. Dad's next stop on the Roman Mile is of course the very same Roman baths. I have seen them many times before, yet they have not lost their glamour.

Dad and I turn into kids, climbing up and down on the rocks, taking risks as we hop from one side to another. It fills my heart with joy to see Dad, at sixty years old, leaping somewhat carefully from one big rock to the other. I take a couple of photos with my phone without him noticing.

"Let's not cause ourselves to be in a situation that we'd regret. We can climb back down from the other end. I just want this trip to be over safely." He pulls me back as I am about to jump over a particularly a big gap. He means my trip not just to Bosra but to Syria. Unlike my usual self, I do not retort. I step back and walk down with him. I too want my trip to end safely. I need it to.

On one of the side streets, Dad takes me into a massive building that was once a church. I look at the colourful marbled floor. There are arches built into the walls of the church with windows in the centre. Unlike most of Bosra's ancient buildings, this is mostly built with white rocks and marble. There is only one wall built with black rocks.

"This used to be my grandparents' home. This is where your grandmother grew up and lived until she married your grandfather," Dad declares in the middle of the yard. Like an unexpected gift, my dad's words draw a big smile on my face. I look around in utter fascination. I'd never known before that my grandmother grew up in an ancient home in the old city, among historic ruins.

This is also the first time I think of my grandmother as a child and a young woman. As Dad describes where the different bedrooms used to be, I see a beautiful young woman, her eyes almond shaped and hazel brown. Her cheeks are as soft as they were when she was sixty years old. Her smile crowns her tattooed chin. I see my seventeen-year-old grandmother in a colourful dress, walking gracefully into the yard. She looks up to the sky, the morning sun shines on her face and she shouts to her younger siblings to come inside as it is time to have breakfast.

As my eyes wander around the now half standing church, my grandmother is all around me. I feel her presence. I feel her joy at me visiting her old home. Dad tells me that when all his aunts and uncles got married and his grandparents died, the place was left empty until today.

Dad's voice brings me back to reality. He describes his own grandmother. He points up to a high wall and tells me how he remembered her climbing up that wall. She used to sit on top to watch the sunset every day.

"When darkness descended, my grandmother or my mother used to go up on the same wall. They were strong active women. They would call in the kids who were playing down the street to come in before night fell."

Knowing that my grandmother grew up in a 2000-year-old house feels like finding a missing piece of a jigsaw puzzle. Many things make sense now. It explains certain aspects to her personality; her humility, simplicity, incredible detachment from material things, her unmatched generosity and her constant emphasis on human connection. All of these are deepened in oneself when growing up, knowing that we are all passing through the journey of life leaving only rocks behind us.

The houses sometimes tell stories of those who lived in them. But it is up to the living to make their own and each other's life a better experience. My grandmother, never in her life, argued with anyone. She never blamed anyone for anything. She never even gossiped. She was so loved and respected. The people of Bosra sought her wisdom and often called her *Sheikha* (the female word for sheikh). This term is usually preserved for knowledgeable men who teach younger people and lead their community.

I feel, as I stand there in the yard of my grandmother's childhood home, a new connection to this magnificent woman. My soul grows like a soft vine branch and wraps itself around one of her many branches.

"It's time we go on to the next stop" Dad says reaching his hand to me. We walk a few steps holding hands. It is sweet. I love how, this morning, all Dad cares for is me.

The joy of watching Dad in his element and the new connection I have just felt with my grandmother momentarily overtake the pain of witnessing the destruction caused by the war. However, as we walk through the war-damaged parts of the old city, my heart sinks. These ancient intact structures survived for over two thousand years only to crumble in our day and time. 'How much harm are we humans able to inflict?' I wonder.

"As you know, here we are at the notorious monument of Bosra," Dad announces with rather dimmed enthusiasm. To Bosra, The King's Daughter's Bed monument is as famous as the triumphal arch is to Palmyra. This too was demolished by a missile during the war, only couple of years before my visit.

The morning is getting warmer with the sun higher in the clear sky, but the tips of my fingers turn icy cold as I see the broken monument. I stop by the shattered pieces of the nearly two-thousand-year-old engraved rock platform on the ground. My chest and throat tighten. I take a deep breath. It is hard to breathe. I look up at the sky and see the gap the monument used to fill up in the air above us.

I had been told, by my uncle over the phone, about the monument's destruction in one of the battles. Seeing it half standing and half on the ground is like taking a picture on a film camera without rolling the film. The two images overlay one another. Erasing the old picture is hard. The gap in the new picture leaves me lingering over the old picture in my mind.

The ancient rock at my feet is another testimony of how real it all is. Once more on this trip, I stand facing all the losses that I thought I had accepted and grieved. Once more I come to realise how little processing, I had of it all. Once more I am relearning that grieving is never really a finished subject. That 'closure' is a foolish concept. Grief lives with us. We only learn to integrate it into our lives.

Years ago, Dad took me and my high school girlfriends from Damascus to see The King's Daughter's Bed. He'd taken us on a day trip to Bosra. We were only fifteen. We spent the day wandering around the old city listening to his stories and taking photos.

I remember him telling us: "As you can see my dears, The King's Daughter's Bed is made up of two 30-metre-high columns crowned with a big platform engraved all around with intricate plant patterned details. It never fails to fascinate me how ancient civilisations managed to erect such tall columns without electricity! Don't you agree?" Dad looked short next to the column; we all did.

"This monument was built in the first century by the unjust king of Bosra at the time. He built it because a fortune-teller predicted to the king that his daughter was going to die by a scorpion poison while sleeping. Knowing his many enemies and injustices, the king believed the prediction. Out of fear for his daughter's life, he commissioned a sanctuary for her." My friends and I listened eagerly to the story while looking up at the monument.

"On the top platform, a small bedroom was built for the princess. She slept in it safely while the servants and guards stayed at the bottom. They only came up to answer to her needs. The young princess fancied some grapes one evening. The servant picked fresh grapes off the vines for her. A very small scorpion that was hiding in the fruit, sneaked in the night and bit the sleeping princess. She died immediately. The monument turned into a religious destination. For hundreds of years, people visited the monument to pray and give sacrifice to the gods for the protection of their loved ones and for the punishment of their enemies."

In the late afternoon, my friends and I had a great dinner, cooked by my grandmother in her home. In addition to the salad, she made from her garden vegetables, my grandmother had made us chicken with sumac, cheese filo pastry, rice and lamb and of course plates of mezza; hummus, muhammara and babaghanouj.

My friends, like anyone who met my grandmother, fell in love with her. She gave them plants in pots, as gifts to take home. She always grew so many plants in her garden and always gave some away. I never smelt basil or thyme more fragrant than the ones she grew.

Years after that dinner, I received calls from my friends. They cried down the phone as they remembered her smile, her warmth and generosity. My grandmother was killed by a sniper during the war.

"Even if I do manage to bring my London friends to visit Bosra one day, I will not be able to introduce them to my grandparents. It will not be the same," I think.

I look at the broken platform piece at my feet now. I close my eyes for a second. I imagine this piece of the monument displayed in a glass box. There is a picture of the intact monument next to it. A text in several languages of the story of The King's Daughter's Bed of Bosra is put up on the display box.

I see many people coming close to the glass box to examine the artefact. A wave of fury overtakes me as I realise that the glass box in my head is at the British museum. I feel shame.

I kick the rock. This war has made me question every thought and belief I ever had over the years. It does not get any more unsettling. Yet, another more unsettling thought hits me. 'Could there be one person or more grieving the loss of each of the artefacts in every museum in the world?'

"Remember when I brought you and your girlfriends on a tour here? It was a sunny day like today but warmer," Dad says.

"I think it must have been in the spring break. I know I wouldn't opt to go out for a walking tour in the summer heat," he laughs. His voice disrupts my thoughts and brings me back to the present.

"What a beautiful day trip it was!" I say.

"It must have been spring break, you're right. It was so sweet of you to do that for us! You even took us to Mzerib waterfalls! I probably didn't thank you then. Thank you for giving me such a precious memory," I say looking directly at him.

I kneel by the large piece of the monument platform and mime picking it up. "Do you think the two of us could carry this humongous heavy piece into the back of your car? We could sell it on the black market and become millionaires!" We both laugh out loud.

He places his palm on my back as we walk back to the car. It feels soft, supportive and warm. We are both deeply enjoying us being there, just the two of us. It is only half past nine now. The entire old city has been empty, all ours to enjoy.

I always feel this deep connection when I am in historic locations, and of course in my Bosra, the feeling is strongest. These sites are not mere architectural beauty or historic information sources. To me, they are places to experience this longitudinal connection with people who are no longer here.

I step on the roads that were cobbled two thousand years ago for me, for those before me and all those who will come after me. As I touch a wall, I touch the hands of those who built it. When I stand in corners and hidden away spots, I feel the excitement of secret lovers meeting. The worry of rebels exchanging secret information. The giggles of a child successfully hiding here while playing hide and seek, just like my father used to.

My dad's next stop for the day is Berket Al Haj. It is one of two water reservoirs that were dug and built by the Nabateans in the first century BC. Countless times my cousins and I raced running around this big pool laughing. The *Berkeh* lake still looks today as massive as it was when I was a child.

Dad tells me how when he was a teenager, he and his friends used to skip stones on the lake and show off when young beautiful women passed by. I laugh. We walk around the lake in the crisp morning.

I ask Dad when we were going to visit the Roman amphitheatre situated in the heart of Bosra's castle.

"No. Not this visit. The castle is under the control of the armed men. I prefer that we do not see them or for them to see us. Next time you visit, hopefully all of this will be over, and the castle will be cleared. We can visit then."

Although a visit to Bosra would be incomplete without a trip to its masterpiece, the intact Roman amphitheatre and the castle, I do not push for us to go. I too do not want to see armed men scattered around that sacred place for me. I have seen enough damage and loss during my trip. Keeping the memory of the amphitheatre intact in my mind is a thoughtful gift from my dad.

It's 10:30 am now. I ask Dad to take us for a ride around the castle in the car instead. I open the small window in the car roof and climb out of it with my phone in hand. After taking a few pictures, I put my phone away. I feel the wind brushing my hair. The clear blue sky and the sun rays remind me again how warm Syrian autumn can be. As Dad drives us back to my grandparents' home, I hear every black rock of every building on the way back say, 'Welcome home!'

During that car ride, I allow myself to forget that upon getting to the house, everything will be as I left it when I woke up at dawn. I choose to forget momentarily that a war happened, that a war took away my grandparents, many family members, three of my favourite trees in my grandmother's garden and so much more.

"Well! Good morning! You guys must have left so early, even before the rooster woke up, haven't you? Why not sleep in and rest?! It's Saturday!" my uncle says laughingly. He opens the house gate for us as we arrive. His comment reminds me that the only day of the week when the world starts late in Bosra is Saturday.

Dad and I walk in, to find a delicious breakfast banquet set up already. Fresh labneh, fried eggs, Horani tomatoes sliced and sprinkled with salt, cheese, hummus, makdous and zaatar w zeit were among the many plates. The setup is like that dinner my grandmother cooked for my friends and I when we visited years ago. I sit down among my aunts and uncles to eat.

For the very first time in my life, I sit for a meal in this house without my grandparents sitting around the food with us. Now I see how my joy of reuniting with my family after all these years has been dimmed by the presence of my grandparents' absence.

But my uncles, aunts and cousins' laughter and delight for having me back is so loud. I can't but smile, talk and laugh just as loudly. As they pass me the bread and makdous, I receive their love. I learn from them to choose life. I learn from them to live with the faith that tomorrow will be a better day. I learn from them how to survive.

Author's Note

The trip took place on 19 October 2019. This story was written in December of the same year, when Syria was still under dictatorship. Writing about it — especially from a place of personal connection — required careful navigation. The neutral tone was not a sign of indifference, nor an attempt to obscure the realities of war, but a choice made for safety: mine, my family's, and those still living there.

At the time, I chose to centre an intimate, intergenerational encounter with place, memory, and belonging. The ruins of Bosra hold many truths — historical, emotional, political — yet I wrote from a place of witnessing rather than analysis, hoping readers might feel the weight of absence and presence without being led to a conclusion. Neutrality, then, was not silence but an invitation to listen closely.

Now, after Syria's liberation and the fall of the regime, that neutrality feels dissonant — as though it veils truths that can now be spoken aloud. Still, this story remains a trace of that moment: a quiet act of preservation, shaped by love, grief, and the limits of what could safely be said.

Dreaming Beneath the Asmara Sun

A short story by Fatima Hagi

This story is set in the heart of London, within a multicultural community that has undergone many migration changes over the past four decades. Ali is a young British-Eritrean man born in London, who is studying International Law and African Studies at SOAS, and volunteers regularly at the Hackney Migrant Center as a caseworker. Samra is a young Eritrean woman from Asmara, who spends much of her time on buses, traveling back and forth to combat the loneliness she feels in a new city. Several times a week, she visits the Hackney Migrant Center to seek advice on her asylum case and to see Ali. The rest of her time is spent cooped up in her small hostel room, plagued by dampness and mice. Despite Ali's broken Tigrinya and Samra's limited English, they manage to forge a deep friendship. The story is told from Ali's point of view.

*　　　　*　　　　*

On a crisp autumn afternoon, Samra came to the Hackney Migrant Centre. As always, she was wearing way too many layers for the relatively mild weather, a long green coat, a red patterned scarf wrapped tightly around her neck and a worried look that concerned me.

'selam! kemey ke?' I proudly greeted Samra with my broken Tigrinya, spoken softly with an English accent. With a

forced smile, too shy and polite to laugh in my face, she replied '*ezgher yimesgen!*''

I could see from the crimson tint in her eyes that she'd been crying, and was avoiding eye contact with me. She handed me a tattered newspaper and sobbed for what felt like eternity. Her cries were deep and resembled a person who had just gotten the news that a loved one had died, she struggled to breathe and was trembling. I gave her a tissue and assured her everything would be ok, surely after hardship there would be ease. I didn't necessarily believe that but it was what I heard my parents say to each other when they encountered hard times. I think it was a passage from the Quran.

Samra managed to pull herself together for a moment. I looked at the newspaper; it was stained with little droplets of water from her tears.

Every week she brought me a different newspaper, wishing, hoping for any news of her dear cousins whom she hadn't heard from for over two years. Samra's unwavering hope reminded me of my own mother who still scans Eritrean internet forums and Red Cross information boards in search of her younger brother. My uncle Kidane went missing when the Eritrean-Ethiopian war started in 1998, well before I was born, but yet everyday my mother would leap out of her seat a little, thinking her younger brother would walk through our front door.

I read the paper and told her that the pictured boat was being displayed as a piece of art at the Venice Biennale to raise awareness on migrant rights, the headline read "Every day, Six Migrants Die at Sea." Samra asked me if the article mentioned any of the people who were in the boat and whether any of them survived. I had a long pause before answering because I knew what she wanted to hear. The desperation and longing I saw in her eyes made me emotional, it's the same longing I saw in my own mother's eyes. With a heavy heart, I told her no; they didn't mention any details about who was in the boat.

I started working at the Hackney Migrant Centre initially to get some experience since I was studying International Law and African Studies, but it ended up being a very fulfilling role to give back and to connect the dots in my own family's migration history. Every day in the papers I would see yet another boat carrying migrants, capsized in the Mediterranean Sea. Pictures of men who look like me, with Eritrean names would appear on Facebook. I was constantly confronted with the horrors of immigration policies in Europe, and the idea that it could have easily been me if I had been born in Eritrea was never far from my mind.

I was very aware of my privilege being born in London, and being British. But I stood before Samra as a man with Eritrean heritage, with an Eritrean name and face, yet very different to all the other Eritrean men she'd known, real Eritreans who lived in Asmara and whose Tigrinya was never up for debate. Despite the deep sense of connection I felt with my fellow Eritreans, there was an undercurrent of shame that lingered within me—a feeling of not being Eritrean enough and a gnawing guilt for not sharing in their struggles. Here I was, never having set foot in Eritrea, yet draped in an Eritrean necklace and wrapped in a kuta (traditional handwoven scarf), as if these tokens could somehow validate my identity. Perhaps a part of me was caught up in the 'look at me, I am so cultured' pretence that often accompanied those of us who studied at SOAS—a subtle form of cultural appropriation disguised as worldliness. Deep down, I grappled with the constant feeling of needing to prove myself, never quite British enough nor Eritrean enough.

Over the six months we had known each other, Samra told me so much about her cousins Leul and Yonas, it was like I knew them personally. They were Samra's cousins from her maternal side, twins, only five months older than her. They grew up together and were extremely close. Samra didn't have any siblings so Leul and Yonas were like her brothers. Growing up a young girl in Asmara, Samra was teased for being a 'tomboy' because she loved playing football outside with her cousins. Her mother discouraged her from playing with boys since she was very traditional and didn't want the other women in their neighborhood talking, but her father understood her need to have siblings and figured playing football was just an adolescence phase. Leul, Yonas and

Samra were inseparable, until the boys decided to leave Asmara for the great unknown.

They confided in Samra about their great adventure to Europe, and encouraged her to join them. Leul and Yonas left Asmara a few months before her and when they left it was like a piece of her was missing. The twins had just turned 20 years old when they started their migration journey. Arranging their carefully planned escape from Asmara which was no small feat since the regime kept a close eye on young, strong, healthy people like them who would be expected to work with little pay as part of the indefinite national service. It was slavery and her cousins had high hopes of what their life could be if they lived in Europe. Europe was an allusive place to them, they thought it was one big country, a place where money flew out of the machines in the wall, where people danced freely in night clubs with no curfews, stairs moved on their own and doors automatically opened. A fantastical place where all dreams came true and where they could be free to be whoever they wanted to be.

When Samra turned 18 it became mandatory for her to do national service and she was placed in a military camp 500 kilometres from her home. At first, she found it traitorous working under the scorching heat for 10 hours a day. It made her nauseous and, on some occasions, she threw up bright yellow acidic bile since nothing else was left in her stomach. This warranted a public beating from the guards who were trained to keep the order and she was not only humiliated but felt so weak that she almost fainted from the painful lashes. They used a heavy leather belt and big wooden stick to beat them into a life of indefinite slavery. She hated the place and the only thing that kept her sane was the fantasies of one day escaping and joining her cousins in Europe. They watched a lot of English-language shows on TV, not realizing that many of them were actually set in America, not Europe. From my time at the migrant center, I observed that to most of the migrants escaping harsh realities in their home countries, all of the West seemed like one place.

Samra told me they watched popular American shows like *Friends* on Arab satellite channels, which depicted an abundant life of fun and the youthful freedoms they all dreamed of. In no time, Samra got used to the everyday structure of waking up before dawn, enduring cold showers, and barely having any breakfast—a bowl of dry kicha (flat bread) that tasted of nothing. From her elaborate descriptions, I could clearly imagine how she spent her days picking cotton under the Asmara sun.

She didn't like to talk at length about her perilous journey through Ethiopia, Sudan, Libya and Italy, but I have read her asylum case notes many times, it's brought me to tears every time and I am still in shock how one person could survive such torture and trauma. Many didn't make it, but she did, despite the odds being against her. Samra was the lucky one, an anomaly of sorts.

Samra told me, life in Europe wasn't what she dreamed of. "Ali, I didn't know Europe was like this, so cold and people are so unfriendly and everyone is rushing all the time," she said to me countless times. If she'd known whilst still in Asmara how hard it would be, would she have ever left? Surely, she couldn't go back now and she had already endured so much and nearly died so many times. If she went back to Eritrea now, she would be severely punished for escaping the national service. And I think the hope of being reunited with her cousins one day probably kept her going.

I once asked Samra if there was anything she liked about being in London, and I recall her telling me about her favorite activity. She relished the days when she could ride the buses all day long across the city. One day a week, she was given a free bus pass, and she would use that opportunity to take public buses, usually traveling to the Eritrean community center on Holloway Road. It was a long way from Hackney, requiring her to take three buses—the 425, 106, and 29—but she didn't mind because it was the only time she truly felt free. I vividly remember her telling me how she would run to sit upstairs, like an excited child on a double-decker bus for the first time. Sitting at the front was pure joy for her; it was a magical place where she would daydream and get lost in the city's wavering movement. She watched people rushing to and fro, teenagers standing in front of chicken and chip shops in their uniforms, perfectly lined retail shops full of clothes she could never afford, and fruit and veg stands eagerly awaiting customers. From the top of the bus, the world stood still, and all her worries were swept away with the wind. I never thought much about going on the bus. It was something I'd always done and took for granted, often finding it an annoying experience as my focus was on the buses running late. But Samra's excitement made me see it differently.

Getting to know Samra taught me to appreciate a mundane, everyday chore such as taking a bus. The last time I saw Samra was on a Thursday. I read her the letter from the Home Office, which stated that her asylum application had been rejected. She was on the list of people to be moved to a detention center at Heathrow Airport so they could be "processed" in Rwanda. We both cried a lot that day, and the helplessness I felt is something I hope never to experience again.

Just as Samra wondered where her cousins ended up, every so often I wondered whether she had made it to Rwanda or perhaps was deported back to Eritrea. My mother still doesn't know whether my uncle Kidane will one day show up at her door. In this age of mass migration, war, and poverty tearing families and friends apart, it's hard not to cling to the common fantasy we call hope, to keep those we love alive in our minds. I think of Samra often, and I hope we meet again someday under better circumstances, beneath the Asmara sun.

Contributor Biographies

Pingala Dhital

Pingala shares her journey of pain and resilience, moving from displacement to a new life. After fleeing Bhutan at a young age, she spent 18 years in a refugee camp in eastern Nepal, where she focused on educating adults at a bamboo hut supported by OXFAM GB. Initially, she held high hopes of returning home, but those dreams faded over time. She co-founded Voice for Change to advocate for sustainable solutions to the refugee crisis. Facing significant challenges, including threats from male leaders, she and her family were ultimately rescued by UNHCR, the U.S. Embassy, and IOM, becoming the first resettlement case from their camp. Since 1990, Pingala has dedicated her life to serving refugees, first in her own community and then in the USA after 2008. Today, she leads The Mahima Project under Thrive International, empowering vulnerable refugee women to thrive in Spokane community.

Sharif Gemie

Sharif is a happily retired History lecturer living in South Wales. He started writing fiction after retirement. He has published twenty-three short stories, eight flash fictions, two poems and has had a one-act play performed. He likes writing fiction that addresses political issues in a quirky, personal way. His first novel, *The Displaced*, was published in April 2024. It's about a middle-class British couple who volunteer to work with refugees in Germany at the end of the Second World War. https://sharifgemie.com/

Marsha Glenn

Marsha is from Bangladesh, where she worked as a journalist. During her journey in the UK for the last decade, she has been forced to identify herself as an asylum seeker, foreigner, job snatcher and public liability. Whereas, Marsha relentlessly pursues to regain her identity as resilient, thinker, activist, compassionate and grateful for the life she has made in the UK. She is a member of the Freedom from Torture creative writing group Write to Life. She has worked with journalist and writer Simon Hattenstone and the Guardian during her involvement in the 'Refugee Journalism Project 2018-2019.' Marsha regularly contributes to Freedom from Torture online publications. She was published in *Welcome to Britain: An Anthology of Poems and Short Fiction in 2023*. She has been published in the Exiled Writers Ink and the Guardian online feature section.

Fatima Hagi

Fatima is a writer, workshop/retreat facilitator and creative communications specialist. She is the contributing editor in the book: *Resistance - Voices of Exiled Writers*, published by Palewell Press. Fatima is currently working on her debut poetry collection and a children's book series, whilst raising an adorable baby boy.

Anba Jawi

Born in Baghdad, Anba studied Geology at the University of Baghdad – one of the pioneering women geologists in Iraq. She gained her PhD from UCL London. She worked in the refugee sector for more than 20 years and was honoured with an MBE on the Queen's birthday list in 2004 for her services. She writes and publishes in Arabic and English. A chapter from her novel *The Silver Engraver* was included in the TLC *Free Reads Anthology* (2019) and two chapters were produced in a chapbook published by Exiled Writers Ink (2021). With Catherine Temma Davidson, Anba co-translated the anthology *The Utopians of Tahrir Square*, 2022 and the poetry collection *Please Don't Kill All the Poets* by Adnan Mohsen, 2024. And she was part of the team who translated poetry collection *Because Of You* by Bilal Al Masri, 2024, all of the poetry books having been published by Palewell Press.

dima mekdad

dr dima mekdad is a new writer. She is the Co-chair of Refugee Week, Executive Director of Shubbak Festival, and a practitioner in Healing Justice London Network. Her career journey spans clinical research, education, arts and culture. She is dedicated to creating spaces for embodied transformation, storytelling and cultural expression for social change.

Nasrin Parvaz

Nasrin Parvaz became a civil rights activist when the Islamic regime took power in 1979. She was arrested in 1982, tortured and spent eight years in prison.

Her books include *One Woman's Struggle in Iran, A Prison Memoir* (Award-Winner in the Women's Issues category of the 2019 International Book Awards), and *The Secret Letters from X to A*, (Victorina Press 2018). Her prison memoir has also been published in Spanish and German. Her new novel was longlisted on The Bath Novel Award 2023. Her paintings were accepted for inclusion in the exhibitions, Calendar and for postcards.

Nasrin studied for a degree in Psychology and subsequently gained an MA in International Relations. She then completed a Postgraduate Diploma in Applied Systemic Theory at the Tavistock and Portman NHS Foundation Trust, where she worked in a team of family therapists for some time.

Nasrin is a member of Exiled Writers Ink (EWI), and the Society of Authors.

http://nasrinparvaz.org/

Haydeh Ravesh

Haydeh Ravesh, originally from Iran, was imprisoned for political reasons. She earned a BA in Sociology in Iran and later pursued an MA in Social Policy and a PGCE in

England. Haydeh worked as a Social Issues researcher in Iran and as a primary school teacher in England. As a teenager, she began writing short essays and poems in Farsi. Joining the 'Write to Life' creative writing group at Freedom from Torture in London refined her skills and inspired her to explore refugee issues, human rights, and cultural diversity in her work. Haydeh's poems have been featured at the Edinburgh Book Festival in 2018 and 2019, and at a major fundraiser for Freedom from Torture in 2021. In December she delivered an essay on Women's hijab in Iran at Essex University for Human Rights Day. Now in retirement, Haydeh continues to draw inspiration from her experiences to pursue her passion for writing.

Gilbert Luther (nom de plume)

Gilbert Luther feels that his greatest debt is to the young mother who raised him and his three siblings during WW2. He is an Arts graduate of Bristol and London, did military service in Africa and taught in English secondary schools for the rest of his working life. Writing has dominated his spare time. He has run many marathons and one triathlon, helped to bring up five children and studied Russian and Swahili amongst several languages.

Palewell Press

Palewell Press is an independent publisher handling poetry, fiction and non-fiction with a focus on books that foster Justice, Equality and Sustainability.

The Editor can be reached on enquiries@palewellpress.co.uk